A TIGHT GRIP

A TIGHT GRIP

Kay Rae Chomic

She Writes Press

Published 2014
Printed in the United States of America
ISBN: 978-1-938314-76-6
Library of Congress Control Number: 2014931079

For information, address:
She Writes Press
1563 Solano Ave #546
Berkeley, CA 94707

For Julie, my partner in everything

In memory of my parents,

Lillian Kosinski Chomic and Chester V. Chomic

CONTENTS

BAD COP

The countdown was nearly over. Four more days until the women's match-play golf tournament. Par Parker's game was hot, her mental state positive. She'd been runner-up in the tournament the past five years. A four handicap was not enough to beat her younger opponents, who made so many birdies against her that she felt like a beginner again. Teenagers coached by country club golf pros and college players home for the summer belted drives and smacked iron shots tight to the pin. They scooped balls out of sand traps and made it look as easy as placing a napkin on a table.

Par steered her Tahoe in and out of curves on Brown's Lake Road with the nonthinking ease of traveling the route home. She tapped her fingers on the steering wheel to the beat of Aretha singing "Dancing in the Streets" and thought about her best friends at Carmen and Blake's twentieth-anniversary party, moments ago, hugging her good-bye and saying, "Good luck. This is your year."

The vacant road made her feel as if she owned the night.

"Par, I'm gonna be sick." The voice of Nick, the husband, in the backseat.

"Oh, hon, we're almost home. Hang on for another mile." Par sped up to forty-five, still taking the curves smoothly. She heard retching from the backseat, smelled vomit, remembered her short irons were on the floor. "Nick! Don't throw up on my grips. Please don't ruin them for next week."

He mumbled, "No . . . I didn't . . . got the metal."

Par pressed hard on the button to open all the windows. Her gag reflex gave her little respect for the last stop sign before home. She glanced left, saw no cars, turned right, and gunned the engine.

A hundred yards later, a siren screamed.

"Damn," Par said. Pulling over, she looked at her side mirror just as the cop's searchlight flicked on. She fished in her purse for lipstick to freshen the color. She pulled out a stick of Juicy Fruit gum and quickly chewed the stiffness out of it. Smacking her lips twice, she said to Nick, "I'll get us out of this."

Par stepped out of the car and saw a human hulk lumbering toward her. Blinded by the wattage coming from the squad car, she looked away and leaned casually on the side of the Tahoe.

"Get back in the car," the hulk said as it morphed into a female deputy.

Par knew her lipstick and flirtation skills would not help. She tried a different approach. "I'm only a block from home. Did I do something wrong?"

"Show me your driver's license and registration."

Par got in her car and retrieved what the deputy wanted.

"That your husband?" the deputy asked, with a flick of her head toward the backseat, toward the lump of Nick Swink.

"Afraid so. You want him?" Par hoped levity might be effective.

"It smells awful here." She grabbed Par's arm. "Step away from your vehicle."

"Anything you say." Then Par hissed into the backseat's window, "Nick. Sit up. I'll be right back."

He moaned, "I'm sorry."

"Yes, you are."

The deputy tightened her grip on Par's arm. "Let's go," she ordered, and they walked the thirty yards to her car.

Par breathed in the night air more deeply than ever before. She considered how much she had drunk at the party. Two cocktails. How she loved the crisp tartness of a lime-rimmed glass full of tonic laced with gin. It was a drink to cut through the heat and humidity. July was the month in Michigan when eyes got stung by salt, the grip of a golf club was slick with palm sweat, and clothes had to be changed at least twice a day.

"Stand here," the deputy said.

Par stood erect between the squad car's headlights. She thought she had eaten enough chicken satay, chips with dip, and chocolate cake to keep her sober. Midparty, an anniversary toast to Carmen and Blake had added a flute of champagne to the mix.

The searchlight switched off.

"Jane Parker-Swink. Class of '72."

Par whipped her head to face this comment, which felt like an accusation. Everyone called her by the nickname Par.

The deputy faced her.

"Dee Dee," Par said, with a hint of glee. Dee Dee Virgil had sat next to Par in tenth-grade algebra class and had cheated off Par's exams. She had buck teeth and bangs that were always cut too short. The kids called her Doe-Doe Virgin. Her mother was a big-chested, big-hipped waitress who worked at the Big Boy restaurant north of town. Pearl Virgil had a habit of sleeping with her customers, and her reputation made Dee Dee a sullen, prudish loner.

Deputy Dee Dee smirked and removed a penlight from her shirt pocket. She pointed the light into Par's eyes and told her to track it as she moved it up, down, from side to side.

"Now pick up this dime." Dee Dee dropped the coin.

Bending to retrieve it, Par skimmed her fingertips along the road's surface, finding gravel, leaves, and twigs, touching sticky lumps and rough ridges of who-knows-what, grasping no tiny dime. "I need some light. I think it rolled under the car."

"You're taking too long."

Par sighed and stood, waited for further instructions. Under Dee Dee's too-short bangs, her eyes were shifty Raisinets.

"Your fancy-foiled hair is the only thing changed about you."

"You must need glasses." Par chuckled.

"But you're still wearing it in a sloppy braid."

"It's a French braid, and I like it loose. You've gone all gray."

"Blow into this tube."

"Dee Dee, you're not going to arrest me, are you?"

"We'll see."

Par tongued her gum to the back of her molars. Lips around the plastic tube, she exhaled and said a little prayer.

Dee Dee checked the reading on her portable device. "Just over the limit." And here, she smiled.

Par saw a flash of braces and noticed her buck teeth weren't so buck anymore.

"I've busted a few of our classmates who were popular like you."

"And it feels good to you, doesn't it?" Stupid comment, Par knew.

Dee Dee's expression soured. She spun Par around, slammed her torso onto the hood, cuffed her, and stuffed her into the backseat.

These actions took seconds. Dee Dee's strength and swiftness knocked the wind out of Par. The seat was hard plastic; a Plexiglas barricade separated the criminal from the law. The tightly closed windows created a suffocating vibe. Sweat dripped down the sides of Par's face. She glared at the deputy's back as Dee Dee walked toward the Tahoe, and sensed evil in her swagger.

Dee Dee and Nick had a conversation. His brawn and height towered over the deputy. He looked toward the squad car, shading his eyes from the lights. Par's thoughts skipped around from hoping Nick did not get arrested to resolving never to be his designated driver again to planning to beg for a warning. That would be as low as she could stoop.

Dee Dee raised her arms high to his shoulders and turned him around. Nick began walking west on Kimmel Road. Par's front teeth bit into her lower lip, and she tasted sweat, which somehow calmed her. *She's letting him go. Time to beg. Be honest with her.* Par gave herself instructions, like a coach.

"I sent your husband home," Dee Dee said, after returning to the car.

"I hope he makes it. Dee Dee, I'm sorry. This will never happen again."

Dee Dee shifted in her seat, tilted her head toward Par.

"Maybe I drank more and ate less at the party because today would have been my father's seventieth birthday. I still miss him so much." She almost added, *He was murdered, you remember,* but held back, knowing Dee Dee knew this; everyone in town knew what had happened to her father. Henry Parker had been the benevolent owner of Parker Chevrolet—handsome, prematurely gray, stocky and strong like a pickup truck. Par looked out the window. She saw her father's face. The one dimple on his left cheek winked at her as she envisioned him talking about new Camaros he had on order.

Dee Dee twisted in the seat to look at Par. Her back cracked.

Par refocused. "Dee Dee, I did roll through the stop sign, but I was careful to look both ways. Nick was sick. I had to get him home. Couldn't you give me a break?"

Dee Dee sighed and looked at her notes. The effort showed consideration. Par felt hopeful.

"No warning. This is my job."

"No, this is your power trip."

"Ha! And I hate that tan of yours," Dee Dee yelled, and turned on her siren. She whipped the steering wheel for a U-turn and drove downtown like a maniac.

* * *

After what seemed like three hours in the holding cell, Par Parker realized life as she knew it was as over as yesterday. The cell's hard surfaces reminded her of her new kitchen with the granite countertop and Spanish-tile floor. Unforgiving surfaces. Any breakable container that was dropped could not bounce for a second chance.

Par looked at her left hand, sans wedding ring. She hadn't taken the ring off in twenty years. In its place was a strip of golf ball–white flesh. A jailer wearing brown-and-tan fatigues, his last name, Bolton, embroidered in black thread above his left shirt pocket, had packed her personal belongings—earrings, ring, necklace, watch, wristlet, keys—in a ziplock bag like leftover scraps. She looked up at the softball-size dome camera in one high corner of the cell and steeled herself against crying. She didn't want to cry in public because she didn't like what crying did to her squinty eyes. They'd puff up and appear closed, except for a shred of azure. Being watched, she felt self-conscious about her nervous habit of twisting buttons off clothes.

Because of Nicholas Dalehurst Swink—the heavy drinker, mama's boy, reluctant carpenter—Par was locked in an eight-by-eight cell, staring at the outline of cinder blocks and wishing the lights would turn off. At the party, Nick had acted his usual self. Not a mean or merry drunk, he had leaned against a wall and watched people, listened to anyone nearest him, talked if spoken to, and wanted to be the last to leave. She knew why he drank so much, was partly to blame.

A jailer slid aside the panel of the small barred window to peek into Par's cell. His tongue licked one end of his black mustache. Their eyes connected for two seconds; then he closed her off from the outside world. She felt like a caged animal and she felt unclean. The underarms of her yellow silk blouse were damp with sweat and emitted the stink of stress. She went to the metal sink next to the metal toilet to wash her face. Shaking her hands dry, she sat on the bench and thought about what Pete Masterson had told her about making arrests. Pete had been a deputy, a personal trainer, her lover in her first and only extramarital affair. He'd told her it didn't happen like the movies, where the cop placed his hand on the perp's head and gently guided the person into the backseat. Pete had claimed, "I don't like to touch people. I especially don't like to touch their hair. When I arrest someone and know they're going to jail, they seem dirty to me."

She scowled thinking about Nick lying on top of five-hundred-count lavender cotton sheets under their king-size bed's canopy, his head flattening a goose-down pillow, his snores mixing with fresh air coming in through a wall of raised windows. His mouth would be open like a chorus boy's, body stretched out like a snow angel, still dressed in khaki shorts and an untucked plaid shirt.

Trying to gain some comfort, Par lay down on the concrete bench on her right side, the hardness pressing into hip bone and ribs. Turning gently onto her back, Par stared at the ceiling and twisted a fused-glass half-ball button on her blouse. She stood up. She paced. She flicked a glare at the camera and muttered, "I don't belong in jail. Dee Dee had it in for me." Par scored an X with her fingernail into a fat mosquito bite she'd been scratching on her thigh. "I'm a law-abiding citizen." Futile words evaporated into the fusty air.

Sitting down, she lifted up her knees, wrapped arms around shins, stared at the floor, and thought of her mother; her sons, Todd and Joey; her golf buddies and fans; and Dr. Ed Murphy, a best friend of the family. She thought of the hundreds of third graders she had taught over the years, knew they'd be shocked and confused if they found out she'd been arrested and spent time in a cell that had once held, and would hold again, murderers, thieves, prostitutes, child abusers, drug addicts. She shivered. But how could they find out? She'd not tell a soul. Except for her three best friends, of course.

Her stomach ached with dread at the possibility that information about this arrest would be printed in the Jackson *Citizen Patriot,* a newspaper that had been kind to her over the years, displaying articles with pictures of her golf wins, and sympathetic comments about her losses in local and state tournaments. People wouldn't understand. They'd think she had a drinking problem and was a danger on the roads, a danger to the community. But they wouldn't print it. Or, would they? If they did, would they use her full name, Jane Harriet Parker-Swink, as if she were a common criminal? She hated her middle name and didn't use her husband's surname, except on legal documents. She thought Swink sounded like a poorly hit golf shot.

Would they put her mug shot in the paper? She realized how entrenched in her cheery facade she had become, realized the depth of her falseness when the camera flashed to take her picture and she smiled, smiled as automatically as she smacked a mosquito sucking her blood.

SMALL-TOWN CELEBRITY

Restless and uncomfortable, Par craved an activity that would settle her mind for sleep: reading a cookbook or swimming nude in her backyard pool. She remembered when she was thirteen years old. Her parents had gone to Detroit for a General Motors award dinner and left Joy, her older sister, "in charge" for the first time in their lives. They were lying on lounge chairs, eating cashews, and sipping Cokes. It was close to midnight when Joy complained about the heat and got up to turn the light on in the pool.

"Let's skinny-dip!" Joy said.

"No. I don't want to."

"I dare you. Don't be a little chicken."

Par's body tensed with defensiveness. She watched Joy strip off her bikini, watched her lithe body cut a perfect shallow dive, watched her long shadow in a few breaststrokes glide to the deep end and flip-turn to swim another length. Par deliberately stripped shyness and swimsuit off and dove into the pool. The caress of water over body parts that had always been closed off from this pleasure made her think Joy had the best ideas in the universe.

Years later, when Par had her own built-in swimming pool, she made a practice of swimming nude every day from April through September; she became European in her views of nudity, saying, "It's just a body, and there are only two genders. Everyone knows what the parts look like." Par's mother had one thought about skinny-dipping: chlorine up one's vagina would cause infertility. Par had loved proving her wrong.

* * *

Another jailer peeked in on Par. He was bald and blue-eyed. His action of sliding the window's panel reminded her of confession. She forced a smile and stopped twirling a button. He shut the door without listening to her sins or offering absolution. She hated them looking in at her. Were they afraid she'd become Houdini and escape? An escape artist, she could never be. She hadn't escaped the grief of her father's death in twenty years. She had married Nick for comfort one year after the murder. Comfort, not the best foundation for marriage, had turned into an edgy insouciance, which Par had momentarily sidestepped when her affair with Pete began. She could not escape her discontent about the growing independence of her two teenage sons—she liked mothering them, loved the nurturing role of feeding, guiding, disciplining, worrying, caring, and applauding.

The door opened again. No knock. No privacy.

The jailer's blue eyes roamed the cell. He was very tan. His biceps and pecs bulged through his shirt. The letters of his name, SAWYER, stretched wide above his breast pocket. He stepped into the cell, shoved the door closed, placed an index finger to his lips.

Par tensed, gave him a slit-eyed look, and pushed her back into the wall.

"You're the golfer, right?"

Par relaxed a little. "Yes."

"I know you hate being here." His eyes focused on her toes. "If it's any consolation, I wouldn't have brought you in."

"Really?"

"A warning, for sure."

"Will you tell that to the judge?"

"No, ma'am. I mean, what's done is done. Your deputy holds the record for DUI arrests six months in a row."

"Great."

"Yeah, she's proud of it. But between you and me, nobody likes her."

"Between you and me, no one liked her in high school either."

He smirked and nodded, turned to leave, then swiveled to face her and blurted, "I'm a golfer, too. Addicted to the game. Even lost my wife over it." He shook his head. "I can't seem to break eighty-five."

"How long have you been playing?"

"Four years. I play six days a week. That's why I work nights." He again turned to leave, changed his mind, and asked, "You ever have trouble with a slice?"

"No, I'm lucky. I hit a straight ball." Par fidgeted. She didn't like to talk golf, but Sawyer wasn't going anywhere.

"Do you know how to correct it?" he asked.

"Sorry, I'm a player, not a teacher. I used to analyze swings, and I could identify what was wrong, but then I absorbed what was wrong into my swing."

"Really?"

"Yes, and it made me crazy. Now I don't even watch people swing. I'd recommend you take a lesson from Johnny Mitchell, the pro at Cascades Golf Course. If it's daylight, he's there."

He went up on his toes, all excited. "Maybe I'll call him today. Thanks, Par."

She weakly mimicked his thumbs-up gesture as he left. She liked that he'd called her Par. When she was sixteen years old, she won the Jackson County women's match-play tournament. The first day, qualifying day, she shot an even par round for medalist honors, hence her nickname. She had beaten older, seasoned players each day that week to set a record, which still stood, as the youngest player ever to win the tournament.

Her success in that golf tournament changed her life. It attracted attention from her workaholic father, who loved the free publicity of the Parker name in print. That week she discovered the ritual of neighbors, relatives, strangers, friends of her parents, and loyal Chevy customers clipping her write-ups out of the newspaper and mailing them to her with congratulatory notes. Casey Carter, a sportswriter, wrote about her potential for making the LPGA tour. The veteran golfers welcomed her to their postgolf parties at the nineteenth hole to shake her hand, pat her on the back, and toast her with beers and cocktails. The compliments and taste of fame were sweet; admiration from her father, the unexpected gift.

* * *

The quiet returned to the cell, and it felt threatening, so unlike the quiet in her home, or church, or within a gallery watching a golf match. She wished for the sounds of birds chirping at her feeders, or a baseball smacking into Nick's and Joey's mitts.

Joey, her youngest boy, her outdoor boy, and occasionally, she'd admit, her favorite boy. Thoughts of him pushed her needs aside. He resembled Par's father, with pale-green eyes, thick black hair, a cleft at his chin. He'd soon wake up eager to leave for his annual three-day camping trip canoeing down the Au Sable River. She always inspected his duffel bag and repacked for him. She wanted to fix him his favorite breakfast of bacon and waffles and watch him eat it in three seconds and then take him to the drop-off point, the Shell gas station where I-94 and US 127 intersected, by nine o'clock. It was a tradition. He'd be around for only one more summer before following his brother, Todd, to college.

Par paced in a circle, pulled on her plastic identification wristband, furiously twisted a button off her blouse, and threw it against the wall. She felt like a bad mother and rueful beyond repair. If she didn't get home on time, she knew Joey wouldn't pack his allergy medicine, sunscreen, first-aid kit, and water shoes, and no way would he pack extra underwear.

A jailer with a well-coiffed Afro and a mostly gray goatee, over six feet tall, half-entered her cell. Par stood still for the man named Matthews. A middle button fell off her blouse and rolled onto the floor near his left combat boot. He stepped on it as he shifted his feet, and she heard the crunch. He didn't seem to notice.

"How you doin'?" he asked, while looking at her knees.

"Terrible. When can I leave?"

"You're in here a minimum of six hours. Then it depends on how many arraignments are in front of you. I'm guessing you'll be out by noon."

Way too late for Joey's drop-off. "Can I make a phone call?"

"You can make as many as you like. The phone's out here on the wall." His guttural voice filled the cell. His boot held the door open, and she walked out.

As he shackled her left wrist to the screw eye on the wall near the phone, he said, "Sorry. Standard procedure."

Humiliated at being treated like a dangerous criminal, she ground her teeth so she wouldn't cry and dialed with her free hand, the phone cradle wedged between ear and shoulder. She worried that Joey would answer and she'd have to explain or lie about why she wasn't home. At that moment, she empathized with teenagers when they got into trouble and faced a showdown with their parents.

Twelve rings. No answer. The males in her home were sound sleepers. Par tried to change hands with the phone. The handcuff dragged over her wrist bone. She grimaced. The painful restraint made her want to scream. *Control,* she thought. *Have some control.* She counted eight more rings, then heard Joey say, "Ullow," in his sleep-drenched voice. She hung up.

"Damn. Nick's passed out," she grumbled. Her resolve to be calm dissolved with the thought that these jailers did not know they had locked up the wrong person. Nick was the boozer. She yanked her left arm, again felt the unyielding steel of the cuff, and leaned her shoulder into the wall. Tears welled, and rapid blinking made them spill. Wiping her cheeks with her palm, Par was distracted by a thin man with jaundiced skin and patches of baldness who was being fingerprinted twelve feet away. He jerked a look at her and with fury in his eyes yelled, "You motherfucking whore!"

Par flinched. Her face flushed.

The jailer Bolton instantly cuffed him. The man continued to spew invectives. His body twisted with rage as he was dragged away.

Par's sweaty hands shook. She dropped the phone.

Matthews came close, gave her the handset, and kindly said, "Don't worry about him. He's all blow. Wouldn't have the strength to harm anyone."

"Thank you." She dug deep for courage to focus and redial.

"Yellow," Nick mumbled in a hoarse voice.

"Nick. You've got to take Joey to his drop-off this morning and cover for me. Say I had to stay over at Carmen's and help her clean up, and say something like you insisted on taking him yourself. Call it a father-son thing."

"Whoa . . . man . . . let me wake up a sec, hon. Are you all right?"

"No. I'm not all right. My God, I'm handcuffed to a wall calling you right now." Her voice trembled.

"Handcuffed to a wall? Jesus, I'm sorry. It should be me in there."

Unable to speak, she sniffled.

"What time can I pick you up?"

She breathed deeply to gather strength. "First, get Joey to the Shell station across from Jackson Crossing by nine."

"Yeah, I will. I'll be late for work, but no sweat."

Right. That's never any sweat for Nick, Par thought. "I'll call you on your cell phone when I know the time of my arraignment. You need to pick me up right after."

"I'll be there. You can count on me."

"I have no choice."

"Mom, what happened?" Joey was on the other extension.

Shocked, Par absorbed an anxious silence and turned to face the wall. Her defenses assembled, then disassembled, and she said, "Honey, I had a few drinks last night. Your father got sick in the backseat. I rolled through a stop sign and got pulled over." She paused. "I'm in jail. It's a terrible place."

The truth.

More silence.

"I won't go camping. I can pick you up, and Dad can go to work."

Joey knew how it upset Par when Nick missed work. *He's seventeen and taking care of me now,* she thought. It felt good and it felt wrong.

"No, Joey. This is between your father and me. Go up north and have a good time. I'll be all right. I just desperately need a shower and a long nap. Your dad will fix you breakfast."

"I never pack right, Mom."

So, he noticed.

"Don't forget your swimsuit, Joey. You don't want to become a nudie like your mother." She knew he smiled at that, and she had needed him to smile.

* * *

Matthews, the oldest jailer, returned with breakfast on a tray. A minibox of Cheerios standing upright in a bowl. A carton of whole milk. One piece of unbuttered toast. He placed it on the bench next to her. A cup of thin-bodied coffee half-splashed out on the tray, soaking the packet of sugar. He stepped back close to the door and said, "You were Pete's . . . um . . . friend, right?"

Startled, she locked her eyes on his and nodded, and time stopped.

He picked up the pale-green Melmac cup with his huge hand. "Let me get you some of our coffee. This is weak like piss."

He came back a moment later, offering her a ceramic mug with the Jackson County Sheriff Department's insignia. "Folgers' best," he said.

"Thank you so much." Par's fingers shook a little as she reached for the mug. "It's good," she said after a sip.

"Jonathan Matthews the third, ma'am."

He offered his hand. She did the same, and his grip buried her hand. He squeezed gently, and when he let go, his fingertips slid across her palm. She did not know jail protocol. Would they have a conversation?

"Pete Masterson was my mentor and the best deputy I ever knew. It's a pleasure to meet you." With a nod of his head, almost a bow, he turned to leave.

Conversation over. The door clanged shut.

Pete Masterson. She still missed his laugh, his touch. She had thrived on his compliments. Par's eyes filled with tears. She had met him in the weight room at the YMCA. He was ten years older than she, handsome like Mark Spitz. He moonlighted as a personal trainer for many Y patrons and most of the sheriff's department. He had talked to her about private, discounted workout sessions at his home gym. He had hooked her with the line "I'll add twenty yards to your drives." After a few weeks, they had felt an irresistible mutual attraction. What had begun as weekly one-hour sessions at his home evolved into her arriving at eight sharp every Wednesday morning for an hour's workout, a shower, an hour of lovemaking, another shower, then home by eleven with a flush that lasted until noon.

Unable to eat, Par placed the breakfast tray next to the door. She slumped on the bench, stared at three buttons (one shattered, two whole) on the floor, and sat on her hands to safeguard the others. She had no idea what time it was. Her tongue explored the morning-after fuzz on her teeth, spending a little extra time on her two front teeth, what her father had called "the Ali MacGraw overlap." With that comment, he had approved the imperfection, and Par had never wanted braces.

Finally a new jailer, Butcher, entered her cell. He was slim hipped and broad chested and had two shaving nicks on his chin. In what looked like size 18 boots, he crushed the two intact glass buttons on the floor, and, without a sign of friendliness or recognition, he said, "Let's go."

She hesitated, dug her nails into the edge of the bench, felt a nail edge split, and she grimaced, not for the pain, but for whatever was coming next.

He led, and she slogged through the tunnel that connected the jail to the courtroom, her wrists cuffed in belly chains, her legs weakened by shame. Entering the capacious room, with its mahogany pews, desks, and chairs, felt hideously familiar. Twenty years ago, in this same room, Louie Francis Bane, her father's renegade salesman, had been tried and convicted for Henry Parker's murder. Bane, a short man with hockey stick–styled sideburns and a small mouth full of small capped teeth, had been addicted to gambling and hunting, and Henry had fired him for too many long absences.

Buddy Oscar, the sales manager and only eyewitness to the murder, told the newspaper reporter on the scene: Henry had driven into the lot in his vintage Corvette roadster. The top was down. The blacktop steamed. He stepped out of the car to start his workday, and Louie popped out from between cars, stepped close to him like Jack Ruby to Lee Harvey Oswald, and shot him. Louie looked around like a cornered animal, then knelt beside Henry and forced the car keys out of his clenched hand. He dragged Henry away from the car and made his getaway. Henry died a few minutes later. His dying words to Buddy: "He's going to wreck my car, that bastard."

Bane sped north as far as Grayling before being nabbed by a state patrolman. His plan had been to make it to the Upper Peninsula and get lost in the Porcupine Mountains. A whit of justice prevailed—there wasn't a scratch on Henry's beloved Corvette.

Par's stomach tightened when she saw Judge Walter Lyons presiding. His wife, Connie, was a first-flight competitive golfer. Par knew it was only a matter of time before Connie improved her putting and shortened her backswing to forge into the championship flight. She had youth on her side and was in the competent hands of her country club pro.

When Judge Lyons acknowledged Par's entrance, he looked shocked in that controlled way of judges and therapists on TV. His lips formed a soundless *oh*. He addressed her in a monotone voice and serious manner. After he read the charge, recorded her "not guilty" plea, assigned a date for the pre-trial, and warned her to stay out of bars for sixty days, he called her to the bench. Par's humiliation scorched her cheeks. She entwined the fingers of both hands, walked toward him, and said, "Yes, sir?"

He bent across his desk and whispered, "Are you going to win it this year?"

"Pardon me?" She went up on toes and leaned toward him.

"The match-play tournament. Next week. Connie and I are pulling for you."

For a moment, Par ignored her bondage and the horrible circumstances of being in court. She smiled and stood up straight. "I'll be giving it my best shot, Judge."

He nodded to Butcher, and Par was led out of the courtroom. Adrenaline surged inside her. "I will win," she said to herself. She'd destroy the stigma of being second best, a choke artist, loser, has-been, oldster. This was her year.

The jailer walked her back through the tunnel and, in a routine, perfunctory way, returned her belongings. Closing the transaction, he said, "Follow the blue line painted on the floor to the outside."

That seemed simple enough. She could do that. Par locked her eyes on the blue swath, walked on it quickly to get out, stiff-armed the front door, and gasped in the rush of hot air. Sunlight blinded her like acid.

She heard Nick's voice: "Sweet Juice!"

He hadn't used that pet name in over a decade. His head momentarily blocked the sun, arms spread wide to pull her close, legs stiffened for the collision of their hearts.

* * *

When they arrived home, Nick parked his Silverado in the garage and yanked the emergency brake into place. Par moved quickly out of the truck while unbuttoning the few buttons left on her blouse.

She opened the screen door to the backyard, kicked off her shoes, slipped off her clothes, grabbed goggles out of the storage chest, and, as she pulled them over her head, snapped the rubber strap against the back of her head.

The dive into the pool energized her body. She breast-stroked three lengths underwater. Surfacing to gulp air, she began to swim laps freestyle—her arms a propeller, her body an automatic flip-turner, her head a pendulum turning to suck air.

Energy dissipated at last, and feeling somewhat cleansed, Par stopped swimming and sat on the top rung of the ladder, crying, head down and hands clutched at the back of her neck.

Minutes later, she felt a beach towel draped over her shoulders; then Nick jumped into the shallow end fully clothed and hugged her. Human touch was just what she needed. She gave in to the embrace, pressed her cheek into his chest, wrapped her arms around him, and breathed in his smell; the Dove-clean freshness of his skin jolted her back to when he had been sick in the car, and put her in touch with anger and disgust.

Par squirmed out of his arms. "I'm not ready to forgive you, Nick. Jail was an unbelievably horrible place, and I blame you for it."

"I'm sorry. Dee Dee should never have taken you downtown." Water dripped from his beard.

"Dee Dee was never a friend of mine. You know that."

"Yep, she definitely was not in the popular group."

"What did you two talk about before she let you walk home?"

He moved his hand from front to back over his new buzz cut and splayed his hands on top of the water. "She asked if I was still playing the drums."

"Great. She flirted with you." She slapped water at him. In high school, Nick had played drums in the marching band—not one of the cool cliques.

"No, no, no. She also asked me how you and I got together. I guess she remembers high school pretty well." He dunked his body underwater up to his neck and backed away from Par.

"What'd you tell her?"

"The short version. After your dad was killed, you had to skip LPGA qualifying school. You started teaching at my school, and we teamed up for third grade."

"Anything else?"

"That the high-school-clique bullshit had disappeared, and we fell in love."

The long version was that she never recovered to handle the moneymen and attempt Q-School the following year. Par refused phone calls from Dr. John Bakersfield, an orthopedic surgeon, who was the leader of his investment group, which included three other country club members. Her rebuffs made this influential foursome lose interest in her as an investment and shift their sponsoring funds to T. J. Green, a twenty-two-year-old PGA hopeful. There would always be golfers with pro potential around, for Jackson was a golf town. The next summer, Par accepted being a local star—was forced to, actually, as she had lost her length off the tee and guts over putts.

"I wish she had mellowed toward me with your story," Par said.

"Me, too." Nick stood. His broad head and black-and-tan coloring reminded her of a Rottweiler. "You want to play some water volleyball?"

"No, you need to go to work."

"It's Friday. The guys will be knocking off early."

"You need the hours." Par wanted a lakefront home before she was too old to enjoy it. Wrapping herself tightly in the towel, she added, "Don't count on me being your designated driver anymore. I won't take the fall for you again."

The thick veins at his neck looked dangerously blue-gray and ready to burst. Nick climbed out of the pool, his T-shirt and shorts dripping and clinging to his body, his work boots soaked, and went into the changing room. Seconds later he came out with a towel wrapped around his waist. The hair on his muscled torso glistened. He ignored Par and walked into the house. They had repeated this scene a thousand times: he wanted to play, and she pushed him away.

SLANDER

On a thick-cushioned wicker sofa in the cabana by the pool, Par slept. A nightmare, in which she was running from headless monsters in fatigues, leaping off a cliff's precipice, mouth open to scream, and being choked by seawater and seaweed, scared her awake. She clutched a pillow, searched the room for danger, and realized she was home. A shake of her head to remove the images, a full-body stretch, and the smell of chlorine on her skin anchored her to safety. She pulled her terry-cloth robe tight and relaxed.

As she walked barefoot into the kitchen, the coldness of the tiles reminded Par of jail, and she shivered from the chill. She saw a note from Nick: *Got your car detailed and cleaned up your clubs. I'll be home tonight after a few beers with the clan.*

"Damn him. He'll never change," she said, and crumpled the note. Grabbing a dishcloth, she wiped her Brazilian-gold granite countertop and thought about her rotten luck.

I wouldn't have missed that stop sign if Nick hadn't been moaning and throwing up in the backseat. Who could stand the smell? I had to get home. She swirled the rag around the cast-iron sink and rubbed specks and stains off the butcher-block island. *Dee Dee had it in for me, and she's lying about my being over the limit. Lying. What can I do?*

She looked around the kitchen and decided to feed her starved self, for starters.

From the Sub-Zero refrigerator, Par removed a jar of creamed herring and collected a sleeve of saltines, a plate, and a fork. She sat in the kitchen nook, inspected her potted varieties of herbs on the bay window's ledge, pinched off some of the lemon thyme, and sprinkled it on her food. After slowly chewing the first bite, she ate the rest fast, as if it were a guilty pleasure. Her love of herring came from her mother's side of the family, the Polish side. Adele Minkowski-Parker was a second-generation American raised on Catholicism but nourished by pierogi and cabbage rolls, sauerkraut and kielbasa, pork cutlets and borscht, creamed herring, and fresh-baked pumpernickel bread.

After her snack, Par filled a tumbler with strawberry-infused ice cubes, two slices of lime, and water and drank it in one swallow. Still hungry, she pulled from the fridge two plates of leftovers and ate two herb-crusted thighs and a mound of mashed potatoes, cold—she always ate leftovers cold.

Refilling her glass, Par made herself slow down to drink and digest. She scanned her shelf of cookbooks. "I'm still starved, but not for food," she said quietly, feeling an emptiness she did not understand or did not want to understand. *Maybe it was the loneliness of solitary confinement. The stark jail cell. The giants who came and went freely. Maybe it was the helplessness she felt in being locked in, and locked out of all comforts.*

Par hated sudden changes. She had been emotionally scarred by murder twice. First, her father. Years later her lover, killed in the line of duty. The shock of these murders and replay of a million what-if scenarios still haunted Par. Everyone told her the grief would subside. They were wrong.

"Get busy," she demanded of herself.

Par stacked her dishes in the dishwasher. From the front of the toaster oven, she peeled off a cluster of oval stickers that had earlier labeled fruit (Joey's bad habit). She drifted through the house and dusted furniture, sorted and tossed *Gourmet* and *Midwest Living* magazines older than three months, folded clean clothes in the laundry room, scoured each bathroom's sink, cleaned every mirror. In her trophy room, aka home office, she logged on to the Internet. She ordered a feng shui book from Amazon.com. Par always had the feeling that she could do more to make her house a home.

Next she went through her purse. It was cluttered with multicolored hair scrunchies; two pairs of sunglasses (one with a cracked lens and one with a missing temple); tubes of different SPF levels of sunscreen; golf tees (plastic and wood); sweat-stiffened golf gloves; scorecards from rounds with two or more birdies (she collected these for a scrapbook); a pack of Juicy Fruit gum with a few sticks left; and a well-worn leather Hobo wallet with a $100 bill hidden behind Todd's eighth-grade picture: a thin face with pronounced cheekbones (from Adele), blue eyes (a shade lighter than Par's), long eyelashes (from Henry), black hair, and naturally straight teeth like his father's. Par saved the picture for his exuberant smile, a smile that was nonexistent in his high school pictures.

Tossing out the sunglasses and golf gloves, she was glad to be home and glad to be exercising her "Pringle mentality." Her friends claimed Pringles were Par's favorite junk food because they were neatly ordered, like her life.

She pulled out her cell phone from the inside pocket and called Carmen. She needed a friend. No answer. Carmen was a plump earth-mother type who still smoked pot and claimed to love the creamy gray her short bobbed hair had turned. Par smiled remembering how Carmen had moved purposefully among her guests at the previous night's party, giving neck and hand massages while accepting congratulations and hugs, listening to and chatting with everyone at least once. She was studying massage therapy in Ann Arbor and had been logging practice hours on all types of bodies: thin, fat, scarred, tattooed, wrinkled, firm, petite, large, arthritic, athletic, geriatric, eccentric.

Par left a message saying she desperately needed a massage and that she had news—bad news. She knew Gail lounged on her raft at Clark Lake in the afternoons without her cell phone. And Pinky was at work. Par's group of friends was the one consistent positive in her life. They had all become close in high school. They had shared makeup, passed boyfriends among one another, partied at keggers, played euchre late at night, dabbled in shoplifting, learned their first dance moves from Pinky's older sisters. They had inhaled their first drags of cigarettes and tokes of marijuana together. They had launched themselves into the adult world of college and marriage with one another close by, organized high school reunions, traveled to Mackinac Island and Saugatuck for their thirtieth and fortieth birthdays (husbands not allowed). They sampled escargot, steak tartare, raw oysters, and they swallowed these new tastes with champagne. They played hockey for eight seasons to reduce the boredom of harsh winters, until Gail broke her ankle. They helped one another through parental illnesses and sibling strife, weight gains and losses, teeth-whitening options, husband troubles, health issues, buying and remodeling and selling homes, and at one point, during a particularly long winter, there was talk—only talk—of swapping houses.

Par changed into a peach linen camp shirt, white shorts, and turquoise-rimmed golf socks. In her Tahoe, she sniffed for evidence of the night before and smelled only cinnamon from four air-freshener trees twisted around the rearview mirror. "Good job, Nick," she said, while moving the seat forward. He must have paid a premium price for the emergency cleanup job, and who knew what favor Albert, their car detailer, had asked for in return?

At the driving range down the street, Par paid for a large bucket of balls. She looked out at the range and felt relieved that no one else was shagging. She hated the distraction of high-handicap golfers practicing near her. Something about their dubs and groans and even laughter, along with the advice of a well-meaning father or husband or best friend, annoyed her.

Inspecting the grassy sections at each stall, she found most had a massacre of divots—small and shallow, or large and deep. The end stall had the most unscarred grass, and she plopped down her bag of clubs. Warming up with an eight-iron, she hit several bad shots. She pulled a five-iron from her bag. She had confidence in the mid-iron, knew she could hit it high and straight. She hit it thin; then she hit it fat. Something was terribly wrong. The more clubs she tried, the worse it got. She sliced a few shots and hit some low screamers. She took the driver out of her bag, needing to feel the power of the long shot. *Smack*—she heeled the ball. *Swoosh*—the ball went sky high. Scared, she dropped the club and sat down on her bag. Had a night in jail ruined her swing? Nausea stirred in her stomach. She looked to her left and scanned the soybean field. The look of expansive vegetation calmed her for a moment. On her right she saw a tall, thin man in burgundy pleated shorts, a white polo shirt, and black visor. He set up facing her. A lefty. A lefty with animal-hairy legs and arms. His swing was smooth, and he had a high finish, but a lefty's swing always looked odd to Par. It was Dave Trenton, a good golfer who often placed in the top ten in tournaments. He never won, though, and he wasn't getting any younger either.

Par decided to take a break and say hello to him.

He had just hit a long iron. "Nice shot, Dave."

He set his club down, shook her hand. "Hey, Par. Thanks. How are you hitting them?"

"Terrible. But don't tell my competition." She forced a smile.

"Big tournament next week, isn't it?"

"Right." She looked at the golf balls scattered along the range, squinted her eyes at the two-hundred-yard marker, knew her eyes were getting worse, hated the aging process. She looked at Dave again. He seemed to want more of a response. "I'll get it together by Monday."

"I'm sure you will. I'd try to help, but if I watched your swing, your right-handedness would just confuse me." They both laughed.

She returned to her stall, hit a few more bad shots. Disgusted, she slammed the clubs into her bag and picked up the half-empty bucket of balls. A few bounced out with her jerky motion. She kicked one toward the range and returned to Dave.

"Will you hit these? I've had enough."

"You bet I will. Set 'em down." With his club head, he tapped down part of a divot he had just dug up. "I never win, you know." He stared at the ground.

Par squirmed in her skin. She didn't know what to say to a golfer she knew would not win, could not win, against the young guys coming up who hit the ball three-hundred-yards and had the guts of Arnold Palmer when he was young. "Well, you enjoy playing, don't you?"

"Sometimes that's not enough, you know?"

"Yes. I know that too well."

At the exit of the range's parking lot, Par watched a sheriff's car drive by at a crawl. Her reflexes on high alert, she strained to see the driver. When Dee Dee flashed a Jack Nicholson grin at her, Par's eyes nearly exploded. "Shit, she's crazy."

As Dee Dee sped away, Par gunned the Tahoe in the opposite direction but quickly reminded herself to drive the speed limit, and with both hands closed tightly around the steering wheel, she felt a little more in control. Her cell rang out with "Dancing in the Street." She pulled into a driveway to take the call.

"What's up, Par?" Carmen asked.

"Oh, I spent the night in jail, my golf swing is broken, and I'm disgusted with Nick."

"So, what's the bad news?"

"Ha-ha."

"Jail? Impossible."

Par shared the worst details of what had happened after she and Nick had left Carmen's party.

"You didn't seem tipsy when you left."

"I know. Do you think Dee Dee would be so cruel as to lie about my Breathalyzer reading?"

"Well, not all cops are honest. And she was one of those weird fringe kids."

"Yeah, and still holding a grudge against the popular kids."

"Petty."

"Evil." Par teared up; her voice quivered as she said, "Jail was horrible, Carmen."

"I'm so sorry. It's unbelievable."

Par gulped air to get a grip on her emotions. "Something's going to change. I told Nick I won't be the designated driver anymore."

"There's always the Pattersons. They're at most of our parties, and last night only three people chose to ride with them."

Emily and Bill Patterson were recovered alcoholics who took pleasure in filling their Suburban with inebriated friends and driving them safely home.

"Where are you now?" Carmen asked.

"I'm driving to my mom's. Have to take care of her cats."

"Good. Keep busy and drive carefully. Gail might know a lawyer who could help you clear your record."

"You think?"

"Call her."

"Already left her a message. Without you guys, I'd drive off a cliff."

"You would not. I don't believe your golf game is broken. Come over for a massage tomorrow."

"I would love that. What time?"

"Anytime between one and four."

"I'm there. Thanks."

* * *

Par pulled into the long, serpentine driveway of her childhood home on Stonewall Road. Her mother was in Santa Monica, visiting Joy, her favorite daughter. Two weeks, every January and July, Adele made this trip. She'd return elated with stories of Joy's Hollywood life as a set designer and most recently with news of her reinvented modeling career. Par suffered the anecdotes as well as any self-respecting unfavorite daughter could.

Walking quickly through the vacant three-car garage attached to the house, Par missed seeing her father's cars tucked in: his red 1956 Corvette, a 1980 Camaro (also red), and a silver Rolls-Royce he loved driving to Detroit for monthly meetings and the auto show every year. She thought about the irony of her mother's refusal to drive, and how quickly she had sold the cars after his death, thus emptying the garage of Mr. Chevrolet.

The mudroom smelled of cat urine; granules of litter crunched under Par's sandals. Furry bodies rubbed against her bare legs, screaming for food. "Okay, okay," she said, and poured kibble into their bowls at the other end of the room.

The Normans, her mother's two monsters. One Norman had green eyes like grapes and a gray body, except for a white throat and white paws. He fetched sponge golf balls. He would bite a finger or an elbow if he wasn't getting enough attention. The other Norman was a blue-eyed Siamese who ate plastic shower curtains if the bathroom door was left open. He was skittish and a screamer, a high jumper, and a plant destroyer.

The cats purred as they ate. She scooped their box clean, swept the floor, and stooped to pet their backs. Why her mother had chosen the name Norman for her first two cats remained a mystery. When asked, she stuck to the line "I'm allowed a secret."

Well, Par would love to keep her arrest a secret from Adele.

The Normans didn't act needy after their feeding. They didn't seem to miss their keeper either. As a dog person, Par didn't understand cats' independent nature and aloofness. There was no tail wagging, eyes of love, wild barking, mad twirling, or jumping when she arrived. The Normans just screamed for food, then moseyed toward their favorite furniture to rest. She thought the Normans must be special (at best) or weird (at worst). For one, they were from the same litter but had different fathers, and for another, they acted like lovers—walking everywhere side by side, licking each other, sleeping snuggled with a paw draped around the other's body.

Par went to the dining room and sat in her father's chair at the head of the table. She saw herself in the shine of the table's finish, smoothed a few loose hairs behind her ears, and looked around. Her mother had developed a passion for slipcovers, and each chair had on its summer jacket: pale blue with a yellow pinstripe. Par scoffed at the trendy style. Adele had decorated her home with massive Ethan Allen furniture. Wall-to-wall carpeting collected dust and microbes. Par had filled her home with eclectic furniture: antiques in the living room; a denim sofa in the den; red leather chairs and a rolltop desk in the trophy room; ebony chairs with cream-colored fabric seats in her dining room; sea-grass wicker for the cabana; Cape Cod in her bedroom; shabby chic in the guest room; pedestal sinks and tile floors in bathrooms; sisal rugs scattered on hardwood floors.

She stood and methodically pushed each of the eight dining room chairs against the table's edge. Walking to the kitchen, she kicked a kitty toy, an orange sponge golf ball and watched the ball bounce off the baseboard and ricochet to hit her shin. "Reflexes getting slow," she said as she flattened it under her sandaled foot.

In the kitchen, Par opened the fridge and saw a bloated baggie containing a chunk of cheddar cheese turned basketball orange and hard as the floor of the court; a third of a loaf of raisin-cinnamon bread topped with mold; half a banana with its black skin folded haphazardly over itself; a bag of walnuts; a jar of green olives; and two half-gallon milk cartons closed tightly with black binder clips Par knew her mother had "borrowed" from the GOP office where she volunteered. Her mother was obsessed with freshness. She smelled every liquid or solid before it went into her mouth. Par did not like the fact that her kids had picked up this annoying habit from their grandmother. As if Par would ever serve spoiled food to her children!

Holding her breath, Par poured the curdled milk down the drain and put the cartons in the trash. With a dishrag, she wiped the surface of her mother's Viking stove, an extravagance wasted on a woman who did not cook. For the most part, the Parkers had survived on takeout food Henry picked up on his way home from the dealership. Or they ate out, which gave Henry an opportunity to shake hands with the many people he knew, and those he did not, before settling himself at his family's table or booth.

Feeling restless in the stuffy house, which smelled like an old book, Par averted her eyes as she walked past the library, its floor-to-ceiling bookcases stacked with horror books and mysteries in alphabetical order by author. Par attributed some of her fear of Adele to her mother's love of these stories. Stories filled with madness, villains, violence, twisted motives, and haunting endings. Her mother had once said, "I'd like to start a disturbing-book club. We'd read only books that make you fear what's lurking in your basement, fear a knock on the door, fear every stranger you see and many relatives." She said these things with high-voltage electricity in her voice that forced her eyebrows upward. It had jolted Par and made her run to her bedroom and lock the door.

Par grabbed the cordless phone. As she swung open the French doors in the family room and walked onto a long, narrow deck, she noticed containers at each end full of collapsed petunias and geraniums. She went to the railing and leaned her elbows on it for a view of the Japanese garden. Victor, the gardener, must have recently raked, as the wavy grooves of sand were perfectly etched. Adele's pursuit of Zen had resulted from one of her trips to California. Par remembered many arguments with her mother about not getting rid of the swimming pool. In the end, Adele had ruled and filled the pool with dirt, then hired Victor to transform the backyard. Backing up the garden was a thin forest of pine trees and tall elms. Par had to admit she felt an inner calm just looking at the landscape.

Suddenly, music blasted from next door. Pearl Jam. "Ugh," Par said. Her reverie demolished by the noise, she flicked her eyes back to the thirsty flowers. "Better water those before I leave."

Par punched in Pinky's phone number and scratched two new mosquito bites on her neck. After a thousand rings (Pinky refused to buy an answering machine), she picked up. "*Hola.*"

"*Hola* to you," Par said.

"Oh, Par. I was just getting ready to call you. I read it in the paper. Those devils at the newspaper."

"You read what?"

"About your arrest last night. How'd you get busted?"

"It's in the paper?"

"Yup. I just got in from walking the Angel Food Cake, poured a glass of rosé, and settled in to read the paper before dining on my Lean Cuisine chicken enchiladas."

Par had no patience for these details. She didn't want to hear the millionth food name Pinky had created for her apricot toy poodle, née Pumpkin. Her words "I read it in the paper" confirmed Par's worst fear.

"Shit," Par said.

"Double caca. Tell me what happened."

"Not before I read the article. Hold on." Her mom had discontinued the newspaper delivery for two weeks. Par raced to the living room and looked through the picture window that faced the street.

"Pinky, I'm at my mom's, taking care of the Normans. I see a paper next door on the driveway."

"Go and get that paper and call me right after. I'll groom my little Fish Stick while I wait."

Par clicked off her phone and filched the newspaper. Front page, bottom right, there was a picture of Par holding the first-place trophy in 1988, her last win of the county match-play tournament. The caption under the original picture had been PAR PARKER CAN'T STOP SMILING. They had created a new caption to match the current event: TOP LADY GOLFER BUSTED FOR DUI.

What could be worse for one of Jackson's finest golfers? The yips, a shank, a duck hook? How about a serious dunk at the nineteenth hole ending in an arrest for DUI and a night in jail? At 1:15 this morning, Deputy Dee Dee Virgil stopped Jane "Par" Parker-Swink after her red Chevy Tahoe sped through the stop sign at the corner of Brown's Lake and Kimmel Roads.

Par groaned. The instant write-up with an archived photo of her looking on top of the world seemed a vicious betrayal by the Jackson *Citizen Patriot*. "Sped through. That's a lie." Par folded and rolled up the paper. With the motion of Venus Williams's backhand, she flung it across the living room. It knocked off a ceramic pitcher vase, full of snapdragons, from a Queen Anne tea table. Par had won the vase in a state tournament two years ago and had given it to her mother for Christmas. She stared at the broken pieces. The murky water sprawled across the slate floor in the foyer, and her nose filled with the stench of dead, soaked stems.

"The whole town knows," she cried out. Her gut felt empty. Her ego felt gutted.

PORTRAITS OF THE DEAD

The Normans appeared in the foyer and pussyfooted around the mess on the floor. The phone rang, and Pinky's voice blared out of Adele's answering machine. "Par, pick up the phone, please . . . Pick up and talk to me. . . . I'm a trained professional in crisis situations. . . .You need to let me help . . . All right, then . . . I'm coming over." *Click.*

Par stopped twisting a button and stared at a display of pictures on the mantel: Par, standing tall with her college golf team after a win; diving into the Grand Hotel's five-hundred-thousand-gallon swimming pool on Mackinac Island; engulfed in a hot bear costume on Halloween; arm in arm with Dr. Murphy as he led her down the aisle to marry Nick; scared stiff on a piano bench in the recital hall, knowing she hadn't nailed the middle section of the theme song from *Dr. Zhivago;* and, a favorite, sitting in the driver's seat of her father's Corvette. She rearranged the pictures chronologically, gave them a critical glare, turned each one facedown, and walked downstairs to the basement, nearly tripping over a Norman.

She grabbed a cue stick and played a game of pool, striking the balls so hard they popped up before dropping into a pocket. Thirsty, Par pulled out a Mountain Dew from the minifridge and drank half of it while walking around the pool table, faster each time. She loved the drink's sweetness. It had been her father's favorite. For the first time in her life, she thought it was a good thing he was dead, for he'd have died from learning his favorite daughter had spent a night in jail, and a second death when he saw the details printed in the paper. Henry Parker loved the free advertising of seeing the family name in Par's golf headlines.

Parker Wins Again
Parker Leading by Four Strokes
Parker Wins Sudden-Death Playoff!

* * *

Breathing hard from her speed-walking, Par stopped to chalk the tip of her cue stick. "Why would the paper print this defaming article? They should never have done this to me," she said while racking the balls, then scattering them with a powerful break shot. The Normans dashed upstairs.

She remembered with each stroke of the cue when details of her father's murder and then a tribute to his life had spread across the front page of the newspaper for a week. They wrote that he refused to join the country club even though he could afford it, and that the men at the rotary club and the chamber of commerce continuously tried to talk him into it. He played in golf leagues at two public courses: Cascades and Ella Sharp Park. He never improved as a golfer, because he refused to slow down his backswing. He'd say, "I'm too excited to see where the ball goes." He also refused to practice and made the mistake of patching into his swing a tip from *Golf Digest* every month. He stayed a twenty-four handicapper only because he didn't mess with his naturally smooth and sensitive putting stroke.

Par nudged the four ball into the six, and the six ball dropped into a corner pocket.

She had also read that her father was a fast talker, a typical trait of car salesmen. But no one outside the family knew that he made a point of talking fast, often practiced talking fast while reading the newspaper out loud. He said it made people pay attention.

The reporters did not know to write that Henry Parker was ashamed he never finished high school, or that he wore wire-rimmed glasses with nonprescription lenses to give himself a look of intelligence he did not feel. He loved movies because he claimed they gave him an education.

Pinky, with about a twelve-minute response time, burst through the front door and rushed through every room on the main floor, calling out to Par. She had run track in college, as she was lean and fast, like a whippet, but without the long nose. At the bottom of the basement stairs, she said, "You gave me a fright, my dear."

Par glanced at her flushed and sweaty friend catching her breath.

"And that unlocked front door—do I have to give you another lecture about the calls I get from burgled and frightened homeowners?"

Par continued to clear the table, making skillful bank shots and a lucky jump shot.

Pinky was well into her nineteenth year as a 911 dispatcher and eager for retirement (the city had a twenty-and-out rule). Along with the stature of a coxswain, she had a way of intensely focusing and then totally disconnecting. At work, from call to call, day in and day out, she displayed steely calm with people in danger; spoke with a confident, quiet voice to direct a parent of a poisoned, injured, or missing child; and listened carefully to angry or suicidal people.

After the eight ball went under and the cue ball spun backward, Pinky took charge. She took the stick from Par, placed it on the table, and led Par by the arm up the stairs to the living room. They sat on the sofa with no space between them.

"It smells like a swamp in here," Pinky said.

Par pointed to the mess in the foyer.

"Ick. I'll clean that up for you later. Kitties' fault?"

Par shrugged.

"Don't you just love a room with portraits of the dead?"

"Pinky. That's not a helpful comment." Par stood up and looked at each picture: Henry seated, with Dinah, the standard poodle, at his side; Adele's mother, sitting in a leather wing-back chair, hands in her lap, fingers wrapped around a black rosary, and, standing behind the chair, Adele's father, wearing a bowler derby hat that shadowed his blond handlebar mustache and stern expression; Henry's mother, as a seventeen-year-old bride, looking haughty beyond her years. "Mortality," Par said, and looked at Pinky with a sad expression.

"Yes, it gets us all."

After a long moment of silence, Pinky looked around and said, "God, I love a room with no pink in it." She had earned her nickname from her mother's affinity for the color. Katherine King had painted their home more pink after each daughter, four in total, had been born. The bathrooms were cotton-candy pink, the living room tea-rose pink, the kitchen strawberry-yogurt pink, the family room flamingo pink, and the outside of the house carnation pink. When Mrs. King painted the garage bubble-gum pink, Steve King stormed through the house, stuffed four pink suitcases with his clothes, harmonicas, and self-help book collection, and stammered good-byes to his girls. He sped out of town in his Pepto-Bismol-pink Thunderbird. They later received baby-blue checks from him with a Fort Lauderdale address. To replace their father, Mrs. Pink—as her daughters' friends called her—had all the girls pick out their own puppy.

"Hey, why are those pictures turned down?" Pinky walked over to the mantel.

Par didn't answer.

She flipped them right side up. "This is a great shot of you. Where was it taken?" Pinky knew to distract Par with a simple question before she got into the heavy stuff.

"Indiana University. Bloomington. Michigan State won by twelve strokes."

"Impressive margin."

"I suppose."

"Who's this tall-tall gal with you and your dad?"

"Kathy Whitworth. One of the all-time-great LPGA players."

"Oops. Sorry to bring that up."

Par knew, after watching her first LPGA event on a family vacation in Port St. Lucie, Florida, that she wanted to be a professional golfer. She and her father walked down a fairway close to Marilyn

Smith, who chatted with them between shots. At one point, Henry told her that Par was quite a good golfer. Marilyn reached into her skirt pocket and gave Par a gold tee with M. SMITH—LPGA engraved on its side. "Hope to see you on tour," she said, and flashed a big smile.

As Henry led Par to another hole to watch Kathy Whitworth and Sandra Palmer hit iron shots to the green, Par asked, "Could I really be a pro, Dad?"

"Of course you can. College golf first. You need to gain experience and get used to playing against girls from the warm states. They have an advantage over a Michigander because they play year-round."

Pinky sat Indian-style in an overstuffed swivel chair near the picture window. One of the Normans jumped onto her lap. "Hi, Biscuit," she said, and rubbed her face into his neck. She turned the chair to face Par. "Tell me what happened last night."

Par shook her head. "I drove home, as usual. Nick threw up in the backseat. I was dying from the smell, so I rolled through the stop sign on our corner. It was one in the morning. No one was on the road."

"Except for a cop behind you."

"Exactly. But not just any cop. Dee Dee Virgil. Remember her from high school?"

"Yeah. She was listed as . . . let me think . . . most likely to . . . become a burger flipper."

Par lowered her head and covered her ears. "How and why do you remember this trivia?"

"I was on the committee to create prophecies for our class. Don't you remember? We were not nice people. We spent about thirty seconds on anyone we didn't really know."

"That would be Dee Dee."

"Right. I typed them all up. We got the booklet as part of graduation."

"Oh, I remember. My prophecy was 'winner of the US Women's Open.'"

"Forget that for now. How bad was jail?"

"Well, prior to this article, I thought that was the worst of it. My private humiliation-hell. But no, someone at the newspaper wanted to add public slander to my pain." Par felt naked and onstage.

"But it doesn't make sense. Jackson loves the Parkers. I mean, the Parker Foundation does so much good with its college scholarships and junior-golf funding. Who could possibly gain from publishing this story? Someone screwed up down there."

"People will think I have a drinking problem. And I don't." Par got up, shut the curtains. "If I had a drinking problem, I'd be into the beer or wine or whiskey right now. I was unlucky last night, and my bad luck is being played out at Jackson's big-screen drive-in."

Pinky swiveled her chair and opened the curtains. Norman jumped off her lap.

"I won't be the designated driver anymore. Nick drinks himself into a stupor, and I take care of him. I drive him home, put him to bed. Hell, I even speak quietly in the morning and hand him four aspirin with a tumbler of tomato juice, supposedly his hangover cure."

"Have you ever told him how his drinking makes you feel?"

"He doesn't give a hoot if I feel embarrassed or disgusted. Besides, making scenes was something we agreed not to do the night he proposed."

"You hate arguments, don't you?"

"I heard enough of them at home, and I didn't want them in my marriage."

"Remind me, what'd your parents argue about?"

Par sighed. "Dad loved Dinah Shore. The posters of her pitching 'See the USA in a Chevrolet' on his dealership's walls and in the basement pissed Mom off. With the four-legged Dinah, mom called her 'the white hound' and ignored her completely."

"That's kind of mean."

"They fought about Mom refusing to drive after her accident, when she quit the Catholic Church, when she bowled two nights a week, and her nonexistent cooking skills."

"I still can't believe she never cooked."

"On the flip side, Mom called him on his insensitivity to her anxieties from the car crash."

"That seems reasonable. But then, he was Mr. Chevrolet."

"His practical jokes made her scream a lot."

"I'm so glad to be single."

"You see, I wanted a chance for a better marriage."

"I don't see how not arguing and holding feelings back contribute to a good marriage, but forget that for now."

"Thank you. I don't need you to act the marriage counselor."

Pinky placed her hands in the time-out position of an umpire. "I think you will win next week. Your dedication to this goal was clear to me when you quit full-time teaching last year."

"I had to give myself the extra practice time. And it helped. Until Dee Dee came back into my life."

"What do you mean?"

"My swing is broken. I just returned from the driving range and couldn't hit one good shot." She stared at the taupe carpet.

"It's the stress, and you look exhausted. One bad event won't ruin your golf game or your reputation. Give your talent and the people in this town more credit than that."

Par closed her eyes tight. "I'm scared to find out what this has done to my short game. If I can't putt, it's over for me." A button came off in her hand, and she put it under the cushion she sat on.

"Maybe you ought to go flying with me," Pinky said in an attempt at diversion.

Par squinched up her face.

"Kidding. It's just that it always clears my head."

Pinky owned a single-engine Cessna. She had earned her pilot's license in her midtwenties, despite her mother's fears and threats about having a nervous breakdown if her youngest daughter continued to fly. She bought her first plane in her midthirties and became a part-time flight instructor after turning forty.

Par panicked at the idea of flying. She worried about her mother's flight home. The emptiness in her gut returned. She went to the kitchen's goody cabinet, returned with a can of Pringles, and paced the room, crunching the perfectly formed chips.

"I can't believe your mom still stocks those for you. Give me some."

Par shook out a short stack into Pinky's palm.

"Statistically, flying is way safer than driving."

"Spare me."

"I know you had a bad time with turbulence flying into Phoenix, your one vacation out of state with Nick. The thing is, high heat causes turbulence, so pilots expect it, and the way planes are designed, it's a low safety risk. If you sit near the wings and don't have a drink on your tray at the bouncy time in an aircraft, you'll ride it out well."

Par ate more chips and frowned. "I don't think I'll play in the tournament next week."

"What?" Pinky asked, with a sharp intake of breath. "You've got to play."

"I can't face people. I wish I was still in jail. Then I'd be invisible."

"No. You'd be missing."

"I wish I was a nobody."

"Fact: you'll never be a nobody in this town." Pinky grabbed the can of Pringles from Par. "These are stupidly good." She crunched down on several chips. "Listen, not playing is one option, but I think you need to play. Even if you don't win, at least count on some positive press."

"Could you swallow that mouthful?"

"Oh, please." Pinky paused to swallow. "You've got a friend in that sportswriter. The public remembers you by the last story they read. That's what you've always said, right?"

Par placed a whole chip in her mouth and chewed slowly, taking time to think: three wins in her teens, three in her twenties, and three in her thirties. So far, none in her forties, and there was pain in that. "I didn't win once in the '90s. My last win was in '88. I was thirty-four years old."

"The '90s weren't a total disaster. You came close."

"Five years of being runner-up." Par shook her head. "I hate second place. I'm so close. Then I have to wait a whole year to try again."

"Second place is an accomplishment, though."

"Ugh. Saying that shows how much you don't understand." Par clenched her hands into fists. "I'm sure Casey Carter's tired of writing about it. He's been kind in not writing the words *choked* and *has-been* about me." She sat down and slouched against the cushions of the couch. "It's the record of ten wins I want. Nine wins aren't enough; the Jackson Golf Hall of Fame isn't enough." She twisted a button. "I never tried again for the LPGA. That's my biggest failure."

"Don't get mad, but I have to say this."

"Don't say it." Par looked at the portrait of her father and Dinah the dog.

"Your talent has faded. That's to be expected. Even Jack Nicklaus can't compete with the hotshots on the PGA tour now. Everyone has their day." Pinky waited for Par to think that over. She was trained in the art of waiting.

Par scowled.

"You've already set a record with nine wins. Maybe it's time to find something else that will make you feel just as good."

"I cannot live without golf." Par believed competitive golf kept her connected to her father. She feared breaking that link.

"Oh, such drama." Pinky rolled her eyes.

"Do you want to be supportive or not?" Par demanded.

Pinky sat up straighter. "Who's your closest competitor?"

"Georgia Davis has six wins."

"But she's older than you. Forget her."

"There are younger ones who've won it three and four times."

"Didn't Lisa Hardy move to Florida? And Jenny Jenkins turned pro. Then what's-her-name broke her tailbone."

Par nodded. "Molly Armstrong. She fell off a ladder."

"This can still be your year to win. Use your golf reputation to intimidate those who are left."

"Well, aren't you optimistic?"

Pinky smiled, which made Par smile.

"It'd be great if I won. Now it feels like my life is at stake."

"More drama." Pinky touched her forehead with the back of a hand, returned to the mantel, and stared at the picture of Par sitting in the Corvette. "Damn. That is the coolest car. Have you talked to Mr. Ed lately about selling?"

"At least once a month."

"He's going to break one of these days. I just know it." She winked at Par.

Par shook her head.

"I think it's time for an Isadora Fest," Pinky said.

Par felt the thrill of it. "Do you think?"

"A night in jail. This newspaper article. Yeah, it definitely fits our criteria."

In college, Par had a roommate whom everyone called Crazy Kate and who hated her life and read biographies as a salve. Before one of Par's out-of-state golf tournaments, Crazy Kate loaned her *My Life*, the autobiography of Isadora Duncan, to read on the van ride to Ohio State in Columbus. Merging onto I-75 with her coach and seven teammates, Par withdrew into the book and instantly became captivated by the free spirit of Isadora Duncan, whose dancing in the early 1900s was a revolution in itself—but more than that, Isadora rebelled against everything conventional. She lived as a bohemian and a bon vivant; she loved to carouse, take risks, travel the world, live beyond the moral confines of her time; she lived high, and often her excesses were paid for with other people's money. Isadora was extreme in a way that caused Par to read about her with mouth-open awe and think, *It's easy to admire rebels, their egos so secure that they don't care what others think—so easy to wonder what it might be like to live that way, and live vicariously through them.*

Where Isadora danced her emotions, Par's talent was in a sport where emotions were anything but expressed. A golfer had to keep all her feelings tight inside her gut (Isadora would say this was an abomination). And quiet was the rule for the fans. Unlike fans of most other sports, they had to be reserved like the golfers they followed, had to hold back their desires to shout a criticism, or cheer for a holed-out putt, or taunt their least favorite player. Marshals during a professional golf tournament carried hush signs so a golfer could wrap the quiet around her to concentrate on making each shot. The most noises golf fans could express were collective sighs over a missed putt, or a genteel "wow" over a long drive. No wonder golfers were so neurotic.

Two decades earlier, Par had given each of her friends a copy of *My Life*. All four had reacted differently to reading the book. Par was the only one overimpressed by Isadora. Pinky said, "The world needs an Isadora every one hundred years or so, but we all couldn't be perfect individualists like her, because nothing practical would get done." Carmen called her "my favorite drama queen." Gail claimed, "She was irresponsible with money and belonged in the nuthouse."

The biography had served as an introduction to Par's idea for an Isadora Fest. She had told her friends that Isadora could be their mascot, and the Fest a means of escape and release when life turned dark or difficult. The first Fest had been after her father's murder. It had been Par's survival impulse.

Subsequent Isadora Fests resulted from the normal upsets and unavoidable tragedies of life. For Carmen: after a fourth miscarriage, after a weight gain of forty pounds, and when she was diagnosed with breast cancer. For Gail: after her home was burglarized, and after a disfiguring facial scar from a bicycle–parked car accident (before restorative plastic surgery). For Par: when Pete Masterson was killed during a routine traffic stop, two weeks into her mother's month-long coma, after a decade of not winning the county match-play tournament, and when Todd went to college. Pinky had instigated the most, at six: the death of Lindbergh (her sixteen-year-old German shepherd), her divorce, an abortion, job burnout after seventeen years, her mother's remarriage, and after a really bad haircut.

They were like firefighters ready to spring into action, slide down the pole, and put out a fire. The fire was whatever smoldered in one of them, causing depression. Isadora Fests were always a slumber party and offered the salutary effects of friendship, alcohol, food, music, and, of course, dance.

* * *

Pinky left the house saying she'd call Carmen and Gail to set up the Isadora Fest for the next night. Par was hungry; she knew Nick would be waiting for food and knew she'd be the dutiful wife. She drove downtown to Jackson Coney Island to take home Coneys and fries. Par always placed to-go orders at the anachronistic greasy spoon. She did not feel comfortable dining in an ambience that made drifters who hung around train stations (fifty yards away, through the back door) and down-and-outers (people who had only two bucks for a meal) feel at home. People like Par could afford $25 entrees, bought organic food, and cooked gourmet dishes. People like Par dashed through the diner, grabbing their dinner in a bag, not making eye contact, not touching any surfaces, and not thinking they belonged to the same slice of humanity as those dining in; the smells of cooking grease and cigarette smoke, however, stuck to the clothes of people like Par long after, providing evidence they did have something in common with the people dining in.

Par walked up to the counter. The cook had his back to her as he scraped the grill with firm, repetitive strokes. She read the whiteboard's special: Goulash—$1.95; Slice of Apple Pie—65¢. The waitress, with lank platinum hair, pierced eyebrows, and a fine smile, walked over to Par and asked, "Whatcha need, honey?"

"Four dogs, light onions, two fries."

"Six and a quarter. I'll ring you up here."

As with movement in a mirror, they both took two steps over to the cash register.

Par took the long way home for a routine drive-by. At seven o'clock, she expected to see Dr. Ed Murphy buffing a hood or door of one of his classic cars. Traffic was nil, so she slowed to ten miles per hour right before she came to his brick rambler and expansive front yard. His black Packard convertible and green-and-white Bel Air sedan were parked in the half-moon drive. Their profiles gleamed.

She assumed Dr. Murphy had taken the Corvette out for a cruise. *Lucky guy.* Slowly accelerating, she pushed the radio button for music—loud music—and drove west on Probert Road. As she turned left at Ferguson Corners, the smell of the meat sauce and onions overtook her. She turned into Rite Aid's parking lot. In a spot in the back, with no cars to either side, she let all the windows down, stripped off the thin paper wrapping from a hot dog, and ate it while anxiously thinking about the newspaper article. Par turned off the radio and called Jule Gladstone, editor of the paper.

"Hi, you've reached Jule Gladstone at the *Citizen Patriot.* I'm away for the weekend, so please leave me a message, and I will return your call on Monday. Have a great day."

Par spoke after the beep: "Jule, it's Par Parker. Why, why, why did the paper print that article and picture? I am beyond humiliated. We need to talk. You have my number." She figured Jule was cruising Lake Michigan with Matey, her schipperke. She moored her thirty-foot sailboat in Saugatuck.

Next she called Hair Haven Salon to leave a message canceling her appointment for the next day. Her hairdresser was a big gossip. Par knew that the juiciest gossip tomorrow would be about her, and she couldn't bear it.

Fireflies blinked light-green dots in the warm night air. She slowly ate another dog and most of the fries.

* * *

Nick's drumming in the basement filled the house with a vibrancy Par either enjoyed or detested, depending on her mood. She listened for a moment and heard repetitive flam taps, one of the rudiments of drumming, which meant he had just begun his warm-up. It was loud, too loud. He had removed the neoprene practice pads that muted the sound. The sticking pattern of his rolls and diddles and drags aggravated her nerves. She reached through the door at the top of the stairs and turned off the lights. The drumming stopped. She relaxed a little. She knew he'd be upstairs in a flash, this act being one of their calls to dinner.

Par avoided the basement. It was Nick's place. His drum set, center stage, gleamed silver and royal blue. A tall, skinny mirror was placed strategically so he could watch his form and, Par guessed, practice facial expressions. Shelves held his collection of bucket hats, which had earned him the nickname Gilligan. Par marveled that he could find the hats in so many colors and in such a variety of materials. He had bucket hats made out of denim, cotton, terry cloth, and straw; nylon and Gore-Tex; corduroy and wool; suede;

and even angora. Most had vent holes and were small brimmed. Par felt conflicted about the hats. On the one hand, the collection endeared him to her; on the other hand, she thought they made him look dumb. She never called him by his nickname.

"My parents are worried," he said as he walked into the kitchen, drumsticks still in one hand, a tall drink in the other. His face was flushed. Par smelled scotch.

He sat on a barstool at the kitchen counter and drummed a roll on its top. Par turned her back to him. She pulled a can of lemonade out of the freezer and mixed it with water in a pitcher. The wooden spoon made loud knocking sounds on the thick glass.

"Did you hear me?" he asked.

The air-conditioning was working too well. Par felt goose bumps jump out on her arms and legs. "It's freezing in here." She turned and handed him the paper bag, mottled with grease, that contained his two hot dogs and a few french fries, then leaned against the butcher-block island, each hand cupped around a corner. She fought the urge to twist off a button. "What do they have to be worried about?"

"They're worried your newspaper write-up will hurt our business. You know, bad publicity." He bit off half the hot dog and chewed.

"*My* newspaper write-up? For one thing, that should be *our* newspaper write-up. Did you bother to tell your parents you were drunk in the backseat and throwing up? Is anyone in your family considering what this has done to my reputation?"

His bite had been too big. He shook his head, continued to chew and swallow.

"The paper screwed up," Par said.

He nodded his head.

"They had no right to print that. No right to treat me worse than the average person. You remember when Andy Wilson got busted? No write-up on him until his sentencing. Then it was only a two-liner in the middle of Section B."

He spoke before devouring the second half: "You're right. Why did the paper print it?"

She poured herself a tall glass of lemonade. "Who knows? I wouldn't have been arrested if it wasn't always my responsibility to drive you home. Some couples trade off being the designated driver. But no way with you, Nick, because you get drunk every time we go out."

He wiped his mouth and beard with a napkin, pulled out another Coney, but did not take a bite as Par moved toward him.

"I didn't drink much at the party, and I believe Dee Dee is lying about my being over the limit. She would have given you a warning, I bet." She narrowed her eyes at him. "July tenth is always a hard day for me. I sure didn't need a bad cop added in."

"Your dad's birthday." He nodded.

"I still miss him terribly, but I know you don't understand."

"You don't understand a lot about me either." Nick picked at a thread on the fringe of his cutoffs and pulled it out. He wadded it into a tiny ball and put it in his mouth. He gave her a challenging look—his Elvis lips made thin, brown eyes spraying anger.

"You are a piece of work." They were face-to-face with this argument, an unnatural position for them. She had to get away.

She walked out to the pool and yelled back at him, "I get more support from my friends than I do from you."

He followed her. "I feel the same way about my family."

She stopped walking, swiveled around. "Your family? The same family that shunned you when you went into teaching? A profession not manly enough, not lucrative enough, not brainless enough."

"That's a cheap shot, Par. You're no different from them when it comes to me working construction. You like the money it brings in."

Par knew he made a good point. After Nick's father had become disabled, breaking his back in a fall from a scaffold, Derek, the firstborn, had taken over the family business. He and his mother had made it their mission to talk Nick into working for Swink Construction. Nick had repeatedly said, "No way. I love teaching kids." Par had stayed out of these arguments.

"You know I had mixed feelings about your leaving teaching."

"Yeah, but you still want to live on the lake, right?"

"Well, it'd be nice," Par said.

After eleven years of being criticized by his family for working with kids and harassed for not supporting the family business, Nick had quit teaching. Now he was treated like a respected son and brother again.

Suddenly feeling completely exhausted, Par lay down on a lawn chair.

Nick unhooked the skimmer from a light pole and scooped bugs from the surface of the pool.

Crickets chirped.

Nick said, "I feel bad about getting sick in the car. I hate that you went to jail. I'm really sorry about that, blah, blah, blah . . . "

Par drifted off to sleep thinking about how their lives had changed after his career switch. She had bought tubes and tubes of Ben-Gay and boxes of Band-Aids for cuts. Nick's body had transformed the first year. He had gone from rock-star skinny to Rocky Balboa–muscled. Par loved the transformation of his body. She also loved the look of construction clothes on him—so masculine, so durable. When he wore his tanned-leather tool belt buckled around his hips—pockets and pouches full, hammer dangling through a loop—she found it an incredible turn-on.

In a short time, though, he was hard on the inside as well as the outside. Her increased sexual attraction to him was met with a decrease in his sex drive. He came home too tired, too sore, too drunk, or too distracted by Todd and Joey. They became two passionless people in the same house, living their present as if they had no future. And, worse, Par no longer liked him.

GOSSIP

Saturday morning. Par woke up in the guest room's vintage double bed with no idea how she had gotten there. This was one of her havens, the bed being the softest and coziest in the house. She had decorated the room in shabby-chic furnishings—a pale-yellow-and-cream cotton quilt, loads of pastel pillows with ruffles, a distressed dresser, and a cushioned rocking chair. She stretched her back and skittered her hands across the white sheets. A new mosquito bite on the back of an ankle made her twitch. She scratched it with the other foot's big toenail.

Remembering the argument with Nick annoyed her. The audacity of his complaining about bad publicity for the Swink business. Par stared at the fan circling overhead. Failures filled her mind: the DUI charge; her string of runner-up finishes in the match-play tournament; how she idolized her father and clung to her grief; that she endured, with sorrow, her teenage boys becoming men; jealousy toward her sister; fear of her mother.

Such a list.

Par knew what to expect if her mother found out about her arrest. She'd hear, "You'll go to hell for that." Her mother's religiosity could be summed up in that quip. But it hadn't always been so simplified. Adele Parker had quit the Catholic Church after her mother died of lung cancer at fifty-nine. Abruptly, Mass was out. Meat on Fridays was in. Confession, out. Grace before meals, out. Praying at bedtime, out. When Par resisted, her mother yelled, "Prayers are just wishes!"

Adele pitched or donated all religious paraphernalia in the house: crucifixes, pictures of Jesus and Mary, rosaries, the Bible, holy cards from past funerals, even the Christmas manger and nativity figurines, which broke Par's heart because she had been in charge of displaying them on the mantel and loved staging the scene a little differently each year. She grabbed scapulars off her daughters' necks (Joy laughed, Par cried). For the longest time, Par had felt unguarded, unsafe without her scapular, and missed the ritual of attending Sunday Mass. Worst of all, she believed she was going to hell.

Par stood up and looked through the curtains of the window facing Natalie and Richard Johnson's split-level home. It was a seven-iron shot away. Their lawn sprinklers were doing their thing—wasting water. Pulling the curtains wide, she wondered if her swing was still broken and knew she had to fit in a practice session before the tournament on Monday. She'd focus on her short game; the fewer putts, the more forgiveness for errant shots.

Downstairs, while watering plants, she checked phone messages. Carmen asked her to bring deviled eggs to the Fest and offered a massage on Sunday; Georgia Davis, a golf friend, offered encouragement not to let what had happened interfere with the upcoming tournament; Dr. Murphy said he'd like to see her; and Gail mentioned knowing a lawyer who specialized in finding loopholes for DUI cases.

Par wondered, *Should I hire a lawyer, or is that the sleazy way out? In my case, it'd be an admirable thing. Dee Dee was in the wrong.*

* * *

After a swim, Par pulled a frozen cube steak from the freezer and nuked it. Her father had always eaten cube steaks for breakfast on the weekends; she had loved the smell and hearing the sizzle when he fried it in butter, and she had loved watching his satisfaction as he ate. Honoring him, two days after his birthday, she ate it like he did—shaking out a drop of Worcestershire sauce on each bite. While chewing, she made a mental list of things to do: golf practice; visit the Normans; make scones and deviled eggs for the Fest; buy Joey's favorite foods—powdered-sugar donut holes, string cheese, Cherry Cokes, and bacon (the kid loved bacon).

Cell phone music blared. Par looked at the caller ID. Out of area. She picked up. It was Tony Scarpetta, one of the chaperones on Joey's trip.

"Mrs. Swink, Joey's fine, so don't get excited. We had some trouble today with him and another boy."

"What happened?" Par felt weak, pushed her plate aside.

"It seems one of the boys got a call on his cell. We told the boys no cell phones. Well, you know teenagers—they love breaking the rules."

"Tony, what happened?" She put him on speakerphone and started in on a button.

"A girlfriend of one of the boys called and told him you got arrested for DUI and there was a big story about it in the paper. That boy blabbed it, and when Joey heard them laughing—calling you a jailbird and flapping their arms—he defended you by fighting with the boy."

The news had metastasized. Par felt jolted. "Is he hurt?"

"A minor split lip. They threw a few punches and wrestled on the ground. These boys aren't fighters. And that's a good thing."

"Who was the boy who got the call?"

"Jason Huff."

Oh, great, Par thought—the son of Jim and Ellen Huff, owners of the Ford dealership.

"I wanted you to know this happened. He's more agitated than I've ever seen him, and I'm not sure what to do."

"Where is he now?"

"I sent both boys to their separate cabins. Do you want to come get him?"

Tony sounded desperate for help. Men loved being around kids when everything was fun and games. Nick especially. "Tony, giving them a time-out was a good start." Par had the Fest tonight and did not want to deal with Joey right now. "You could have them apologize to each other and shake hands. Maybe give them some extra chores. You know, keep them there to work it out." The button came off, and she placed it in her pocket.

"I hate it when things go like this. Don't think I'm excited about calling Jim Huff. He's an SOB. My kid's been working summers for him."

"I heard he's a bully. My dad didn't like him at all."

"I guess it might be good to see that Joey and Jason's actions have consequences. Then the group can go back to normal."

"Don't mention you called me; then you don't need to call Jim Huff. Tell the boys that what happened up there stays up there. They ought to be able to rally around that, don't you think?"

"Yeah. I'm glad I called you first. Thanks for your help."

Par hung up the phone with a feeling of satisfaction about how she had handled Tony. But a second later, she felt miserable about Joey's having to defend his mother. She considered punishing herself in the same way she punished her sons—by taking away a luxury for a week and adding a chore: no watching *Friends* on TV, and she'd vacuum the pool.

In Joey's room, she curled her toes into the green-and-white tufted yarn of his MSU area rug. He'd be the one to attend her alma mater. So far his grades were good enough. She put tennis balls back into containers, touched two fingers to the hockey stick's blade on the poster of Gordie Howe (mimicking Joey's gesture before a game for luck), turned off his tangerine iMac, made his bed, leafed through *Harry Potter and the Chamber of Secrets,* which he had left on his pillow, and smiled until she came to his bookmark at chapter 10: a picture of Joey, dressed in tennis whites, with an arm draped around his girlfriend's narrow shoulders. His smile hinted at pride and ownership. Par thought him too young for that kind of smile. His girlfriend, P. C. Morgan (née Patsy Cline Morgan), was a petite, bespectacled sixteen-year-old with shoulder-length dark-brown hair parted slightly off center—one side tucked behind her ear, the other side floating loose. She tilted her head toward Joey, not smiling but looking smug and content.

Par critiqued P. C.'s outfit. Gigantic silver hoop earrings (too big for her smallish face), a peach halter dress (matronly long) accented with her ever-present (like Linus and his blanket) orange-and-purple polyester scarf, worn as a side-knotted belt, and brown ankle-strap sandals (nice).

Par's explanation of P. C. to her friends last fall: *Joey's replaced his brother with a girl. She's a poor girl—scrawny, pouty, long banged, a chess master—who has parents from Nashville who decorate their Christmas tree with beer cans and live on welfare, claiming bad backs and bad nerves.*

Had Joey forgotten to pack the picture, or was the flame burning out? She hoped for the latter and squeezed the book shut. The effort slapped air into her face. *Kids. They have lives of their own now.* She tossed the book onto his bed and left the room.

* * *

Driving first to Drips-Drop-In for a mocha latte, Par ordered at the drive-through to avoid people and parked in the back to drink it, all the while thinking about Joey. He would blame his father for her predicament, and that brought her some comfort.

At the golf course, she focused on her short game. She loved to tap ball after ball lined up four, five, or six feet away from the cup and hear the ball's *plunk* when it dropped into the hole. She practiced her chip shot over a bunker, the pitch and run from the fringe, and sand shots. She loved the finesse of it all. Two hours later, her short game in shape and feeling satisfied, she went to the shag range and hit some iron shots. Some bad iron shots. She tried every iron in her bag—from the wedge to her two-iron. Nothing felt right. The straight, high arc that came from hitting the ball with the blade's sweet spot eluded her. The confidence she had earned on the practice green quickly turned to insecurity on the range. "I'll never win next week," she muttered as she dropped her seven-iron onto the ground.

Nick's voice startled her. "I thought I'd find you here."

She gave him a forlorn look. "I've got problems."

"Who doesn't?" He took off his denim bucket hat, grabbed a towel off her golf bag, and wiped sweat off his head and neck. "Man, it's hot in this open field."

Par looked at the ground. "I'll never win next week, not with a broken swing." He wouldn't understand. She pulled her driver out of the bag for something to do while she fought back tears, placed a ball on a tee, noticed her hand shaking as she did this familiar maneuver, and smacked a drive—a low screamer.

"Damn." She pounded the ground with the club's head.

Nick moved close and placed a ball on the tee. "Try it again," he said.

Smack. A bad slice.

"Again." He placed another ball.

Smack. A worse slice.

"Your grip looks too tight. Loosen it up and try again."

She glared at Nick and lashed out with sarcasm, "What, are you a golf pro now?"

"It's just an observation. Try it."

She loosened her grip and took a couple of practice swings. That actually felt better. She addressed a ball, swung back slowly, and came through high. Connecting with the sweet spot, she sent the ball sailing 250 yards, dead straight. She hit a few more, Nick placing a ball on the tee each time.

"It's back. My swing is back!" She looked incredulously at the balls she had scattered all over the range. "Thank you," she said to Nick.

"Dumb luck," he said.

Putting her driver away, Par pulled out her five-iron. "Let's see if it transfers to my irons." There it was—high and straight. Perfect. She hit a few more. All the same. With a few range balls left and afraid to use up all her good shots, she placed her clubs in the golf bag and slipped on leather head covers. "We're having an Isadora Fest tonight at Carmen's."

"Figures." He slid his sunglasses to the top of his head.

She took off her golf glove. "What have you been up to?"

He looked at his watch, then scratched the back of his neck. "I went over to my mom's and then helped Natalie bathe and clip the nails on two giant schnauzers."

Par bristled. She hated that he went to his mother's every Saturday, thought it immature. "Can you invite Blake and Jesse over?"

"Well, that is the routine, isn't it . . . for your Fests?" His hands went into the pockets of his gray cargo shorts.

"Yes, it is."

"Jesse won't come. He's addicted to fantasy baseball."

"Oh, that's right." She started to rub the dirt and grass stains off her long irons with a wet towel and told Nick about Tony's phone call and Joey's fight.

"Wow. News travels fast. That poor kid."

Right. Poor kid. "Do not forget, Nick, that I got arrested. I had to sit in jail. I had to read about it with everyone else in Jackson, and now I have to somehow live it down. And you came out of your drunken state in a comfortable bed without a mark on your reputation."

Nick brought the sunglasses down to cover his eyes.

"I'm glad he defended me," Par said.

"Yeah, well, he is a mama's boy."

"Just like his father."

Nick scowled, cracked his knuckles. "We should do something special for him when he comes home tomorrow."

"I bought him all his favorite foods. He probably will want to see you-know-who."

"Oh, yeah. His woman." Nick bent at the waist to pick up Par's golf bag.

She quickly grabbed the strap and heaved it onto her shoulder. "I got it," she said, and suddenly felt the weight of their misery with each other.

They walked to the parking lot with a yard of bitter space between them.

"I'll call Blake when I get home," Nick said, before he got into his truck.

He's doing me a favor, Par thought. "Want to go for a beer at the Water Hazard? I'll buy, and I won't say a word if you get their heart-attack onion rings."

"Whoa. I'm stunned by the invitation," he said, as he placed his hand on his chest.

Par rarely went to the Water Hazard Lounge with anyone but her golf buddies. People in her life were compartmentalized, and she found no reason for them to overlap. Her golf league had a long table in the back corner reserved for every Wednesday at eleven thirty. Their conversations centered on golf: birdies, holed-out sand shots, three-putt greens; kids: dating, driving, drinking; husbands: sex, no sex, temptations. They drank Schlitz in the '70s, Miller Light in the '80s, Michelob in the '90s, and Rolling Rock at the millennium.

Nick asked Par on their way in, "You sure you want to be here? Didn't the judge say stay out of bars?"

"I won't drink, so it's okay."

As Par's eyes adjusted to the dark and her bare skin to the coolness, she smelled burgers on the grill and heard a guy shout while playing darts. She loved the place, loved the old waitresses, Doris and Opal, with their bad perms and wattles. She loved the glow of aquariums stacked above the row of liquor bottles behind the bar. The Water Hazard was a favorite nineteenth hole for most golfers leaving the Cascades Golf Course. The restaurant-bar hadn't changed its menu since the owners, Dick and Hattie Milford, had taken over in '65. They had recently printed No Wraps! at the top of the menu in bold red, and at the bottom, No Microbrews! The house specialties were thick burgers, thick fries, and thick shreds of cabbage and carrots drenched with mayonnaise. There had been one change, though: Par noticed that someone had added poppy seeds to the coleslaw. She pictured Opal doing it.

The Milfords loved their golfing customers and paid tribute to them and their favorite pros. On the walls were pictures of Dave and Mike Hill, local brothers who made the tour in the 1960s, and Elaine Crosby, an LPGA player beginning in 1985. There were several other pictures of local golfers who had played the Florida or European mini-tours (short-term stints with humbling performances). A section of one wall pictured three years' worth of smiling women's match-play champions and men's master champions. The defending champs from last year, Hilary Harris and Tommy White, were both part of the group of twentysomethings who dominated Jackson's current golf scene. Different generations were represented with pictures of Ben Hogan, Jack Nicklaus, and Tiger Woods; Babe Didrikson Zaharias, Nancy Lopez, and Annika Sörenstam.

Nick and Par sat at a small table. Opal came over and smiled, exposing a gold-capped front tooth complemented by a gold herringbone necklace.

"I need an ice-cold Pabst and an order of onion rings," Nick said.

"Skip the beer for me. I'll have a Coke with a ton of ice. I've been sweating over at the driving range."

Opal raised her invisible eyebrows, pursed her lips, wrote down the order in shaky handwriting, walked away, and yelled, "Rings. Two PBRs."

Par looked at Nick and shrugged, as if helpless to remind her of the Coke order. "She's on autopilot. No need to upset her."

When Opal brought the two bottles of beer, Par pushed hers toward Nick for him to drink.

* * *

Later, with a Diana Ross CD playing songs from the '70s, Par made lemon-ginger scones and deviled eggs with her secret ingredient, wasabi, for the Fest. She painted her toenails lime green to match her flip-flops. To hide her golfer's tan, she rubbed bronzing lotion onto the tops of her feet, ankles, and left hand, pale from wearing a golf glove. She packed her workout bag with a large MSU T-shirt to sleep in, a toothbrush, earplugs, a handful of vitamins in a baggie, lip gloss, night firming lotion, and hoop earrings for the morning to pair with a lavender linen shirt-and-shorts ensemble. The all-important tunic, she retrieved from her trophy room's closet. She'd proudly wear it to dance in at the Fest. She glanced at the poster of Isadora at the Acropolis in Greece. In an ankle-length white tunic, Isadora seemed to float, her waist and hips forward while leaning backward with chest, neck, and head; her right arm stretched in front of her body, her left arm extended behind her with a deep elbow bend; both wrists gracefully limp; right leg stretched upward led by the tips of her toes, left leg kicked back and high. This movement inspired Par for the dance she'd perform later in the evening.

* * *

Norman duty. They screeched, devoured the kibble Par poured into their bowls. She scooped and bagged and spent more time than usual petting each cat. Were they starting to like her, or was it the other way around? She picked up a Norman and cuddled with him in an overstuffed chair in the den. On a side table, she stared at the picture of her father on his last birthday, blowing out candles crowding the cake's top. Since she had been fifteen years old, Par's responsibility had been to order a chocolate cake with buttercream frosting from the Baketeria, where Lola Avondale, an underemployed artist, squeezed tubes of icing into the shape of Henry's Corvette roadster—Venetian red, top down—and a caricature of him with hair blowing straight back, forehead stretched, eyes glaring like headlights, teeth shown off in a sinister smile like the roadster's front grille. Par wished she could have ordered a sheet cake big enough to accommodate seventy candles and seen him smile like that again.

Par had loved the Corvette. She'd felt like a million bucks being driven around town in it, because her father had felt like a million bucks driving it. He'd say, "Par, count the heads that turn when they see us in this car." He drove down Michigan Avenue, through Cascades Park, out South Jackson Road to Clark Lake, and sometimes they'd go west on I-94 toward Chicago (never going beyond

Kalamazoo). When truckers sped by, the sports car would vibrate. Henry would tighten his grip on the steering wheel, and Par would feel scared being so low to the road when the semis cast the car in heavy shadow.

After the news spread of Henry's death, several potential buyers called Adele. She refused to take their calls, made Par tell them the Corvette was not for sale. Before a full month passed, Adele called Ed Murphy and asked him to take it off her hands for a lowball price—the memory of Henry too strong as she walked by it in the garage. Dr. Ed Murphy, professor emeritus of English from the University of Michigan, collector of classic cars, senior golf champ at the Country Club of Jackson for most of the past twenty years, and one of Henry Parker's best friends, wrote a check that day, eager to add a sports car to his collection.

The story Adele told Par, however, was that she decided to sell it because it reminded her of the many arguments throughout Adele and Henry's marriage. Par never forgave her mother for selling the Corvette. Believing the car was hers, Par kept it in her life with drive-bys past Dr. Murphy's home, visits making offers to buy the car, phone calls, and notes to remind him she was watching. Watching to make sure the Corvette stayed in his possession, desperately needing reassurance that one thing in her life could stay the same. Until the day he would sell it to her, she'd remain a car stalker.

THE ISADORA FEST

As Par drove into Carmen's driveway and parked behind her old Chevy Blazer with a GORE FOR PRESIDENT bumper sticker, she frowned. Carmen was the only Democrat in their group. Par walked around the side of Carmen's house to the waterfront. She looked out at the lake: homes scattered around its perimeter, protected greenbelt on the east side, a fishing boat in the middle, and a speedboat nearby circling back to pick up a downed skier. When the speedboat killed its motor, the quiet and the rippled water calmed her. For the first time since her arrest, she felt the distress over it and the newspaper write-up subside. *This is why we always have our Isadora Fests here,* she thought. Isadora had needed the sea for rejuvenation and healing. Carmen's lake provided the same type of therapy.

The waterfront property had been bequeathed to Carmen by the eccentric grandmother for whom she was named. Grandma's passions had included watching NASCAR races, drinking root beer floats for breakfast, attending Michigan State women's basketball games, and howling with her beagle at the full moon.

Needing her friend, Par walked onto the deck, passed under the sign Barefoot Bliss, and entered the great room. Peace lilies—small, medium, and giant—were the first attraction anyone noticed in Carmen's home. They were blooming in each corner and on tables, shelves, plant stands, and the kitchen counter. Carmen was chopping scallions in the kitchen, wearing a tie-dyed sundress and hemp choker. Janis Joplin sang "Summertime."

"That woman sounds hurt when she sings," Par said above the music.

Carmen dropped her chef's knife and gave Par a hug. It was a tight, strong hug, as if she never wanted to let go. Par smelled onions and garlic mixed up with Carmen's hair scent of lavender shampoo.

Par pulled back a little, and they air-kissed like the French.

"I thought you'd be here earlier."

"Did a quick drive-by."

"You stalker."

"It's a guilty pleasure."

"Will you ever face the fact you may never get that car back?"

"Oh yes, I will. Dr. Murphy told me he'd sell it only to me."

"What about his kids? And what's in his will?"

"They live in New York."

"So?"

"New Yorkers don't drive."

"What about his other cars?"

"Don't know and don't care." Par touched Carmen's shoulder and said, "Thanks for having the Fest tonight. I love being here with our pack."

"Me, too. I'm so sorry about your arrest." She turned down the music and resumed chopping.

"I know, I know. I need to pee; then I'll help you get things ready."

Par walked down the hallway, glancing at pictures of Carmen's older brother, Dean. This space was his memorial, a way to keep him close. Dean, standing tall on the mound as a Little League pitcher; naked in a wading pool with Carmen, hair plastered to their small heads and smiles stretched wide as their cheeks touched; sprawled on the hood of his first car, a white-and-black '67 Ford Fairlane; side-hugging his date at a high school prom; high-fiving the coach at the state basketball championship; sliding down sand dunes at Ludington; wearing full combat gear and holding an M16 at boot camp.

In the bathroom, Par heard a car's tires crunch over the gravel drive. Peeking through the blind, she saw Gail's gold convertible Mustang nudge the fender of her Tahoe. She watched Gail apply lipstick with the aid of her side mirror. Gail would never be seen without her ruby lipstick; her lips were naturally pale gray, which, she claimed, made her look sick. She, their business-minded girl (MBA from U of M), stepped out of the car wearing a lime V-neck T-shirt and seersucker capris. From her backseat she pulled out a duffel bag on wheels, then stacked a stuffed paper grocery bag, a shoulder purse, and a bouquet of yellow-and-white gerbera daisies on top. She walked to the back door laden and resolute.

Par thought Gail was attractive in a neat, well-balanced, financial-statement way. She had full, perky breasts and showed them off with tight-fitting tops. Her complexion was cover-girl clear. Her height, five eleven, commanded attention. Gail rarely talked about her childhood. When she was twelve, her parents had been killed in a car accident. She had moved from San Diego to live with her aunt Phoebe in rural Jackson County. Her brother had already been a freshman in college. The most she said about her parents was that they had been good-looking "on the outside."

* * *

"How are you doing now that you're out?" Gail blurted.

"You sound like I was in for years. It was less than twelve hours, you know."

Gail briefly hugged Par, pushed her away while holding on to her shoulders, and looked her up and down. "I know. Just kidding. You got screwed by the newspaper."

"Right, and I can't figure that out."

Carmen looked puzzled. "The newspaper?"

"Yeah, they printed a small article and paired it with an archived golf picture in yesterday's paper. If you read the paper once in a while, Carmen, you'd know what's going on."

"Don't really want to know. And now I do. You guys always give me all the news I need." She smiled, and no one argued the point.

"But why slander Par Parker?" Gail's brow furrowed.

"You have an enemy at the newspaper?" Carmen asked in a high-pitched voice.

"A sniper. A direct hit," Par said, and immediately was sorry for her choice of words. Dean had been killed by a sniper in Vietnam.

Carmen stopped dicing tomatoes. The room filled with quiet.

Her recovery was quick, though: she simply changed activities, placing the daisies in a vase and opening a bottle of wine. "This is a French cabernet. They described it as smoky, spicy, and mysteriously leathery."

"Oooh, sounds like a man I'd like," Par raised her eyebrows twice.

"Yeah, in your dreams," Gail said.

They laughed.

Par proposed a toast. "To Isadora. A woman who danced, loved, and lived with wild abandon."

"An example for us all," Carmen offered.

Gail called for bets on how late Pinky would be.

A half hour later, they heard two blasts of a Malibu's horn. Soon after, Pinky rushed through the door, wearing a Detroit Tigers ball cap with the visor turned backward, a red tank top with a dime-size stain by one nipple, pink shorts, several silver bracelets, and red flip-flops showing off glittery-orange toenails. She was out of breath and bent over, acting as if what she carried weighed a hundred pounds. As was her custom, she stopped at one of the ladder-back chairs at the country table and kissed Dean's dog tags, which hung around its stile, forever saving his place. She had had a crush on Dean. Then she hefted a tote onto the kitchen counter and pulled out a bottle of *sémillon* and a batch of Motown CDs. She stammered excuses. "Sorry I'm late. Muffin had an accident. Poor old dog. She's having trouble being geriatric. Mom called right when I picked up my car keys. I had to talk to her about my little Apple Pie. Then I looked at my withered plants and decided to water the dear things. And don't look at this stain—it will not come out, and I wanted to wear red tonight." She covered it with two fingertips.

Gail looked at the clock and winked at Carmen and Par because she had won the bet.

They carried plastic wine glasses, the *sémillon* in an ice bucket, beach towels, CDs, Par's deviled eggs, a Costco-size bag of blue-corn chips, and Carmen's famous salsa and guacamole dip. Leading the way on the dock toward her pontoon raft, Carmen hollered a greeting to her neighbor, who had just appeared on his deck. He nodded. She whispered, "Ralph always comes outside when I have company. Watch, he'll start puttering around his Bayliner."

Reflexively, the women waved and smiled at Ralph.

"He never actually takes that boat out."

"He looks like Danny DeVito," Pinky said.

"Yeah, Jackson attracts movie stars," Par struggled to keep a straight face.

"Right, like Antarctica and tulips," Gail quipped.

Though Pinky had already filled Carmen and Gail in on some details of Par's ordeal, as the raft drifted away from the dock, they started asking questions and Par answered: What was jail like? *Stark. The jailers were all giants. I felt like a speck of a human being.* Did they do a strip search? *No, thank God. They did strip me of all my jewelry. I hadn't taken this wedding band off in twenty years.* Did you get hand-cuffed? *Yes, Dee Dee cuffed me as if I were a dangerous criminal. When I went into court for my arraignment, they cuffed me in belly chains, and that was even worse.* Did they feed you? *I couldn't eat.* Couldn't you talk your way out of it? *Maybe with anyone but Dee Dee Virgil.* Why wouldn't she just give you a warning? *Do you remember anything about high school?*

Par pointed to the puffy bruises on her wrist bones.

"Brutal," her friends said.

"One of the jailers was a fan of mine and a golf addict."

"No surprise," Gail said.

"Another was a friend of Pete's."

"Did you get any special treatment from them?" Pinky asked.

"I got one good cup of coffee in a ceramic mug."

As Carmen anchored the raft in the middle of the lake, the heat of the day cooled quickly. Clouds created their own special dark art, and Par expected a thunderstorm any minute.

As the questioning stalled, Pinky arranged CDs in the player's carousel. They each ate several deviled eggs and told Par they were the best ever.

Then more questions: Was anyone in the cell with you? *No, and I've never felt so alone in my life.* Who'd you call with your one phone call? *You get as many phone calls as you like, but it's tough because one wrist is shackled to the wall.* Did you get any sleep? *No way. The lights never turn off, and there's a camera up high in a corner, watching everything.* Do you have to go back to court? *In a few weeks for the pre-trial. The judge knew me.* Probably a loyal Chevy customer. *Right, and I play golf with his wife.*

Otis Redding came on, singing "(Sittin' On) the Dock of the Bay."

"A sad song, but one of my favorites," Carmen said.

"I love the beat," Gail tapped her foot.

"Great voice," Pinky chimed in.

"He died way too young," Par said.

The four women, in a pensive state, listened to the words through to the end. Par sensed relief in each friend—relief that it hadn't been they who'd gotten busted, and knowing it easily could have been. She thought about what it would have been like for them. Pinky had connections. She probably wouldn't have been taken to jail, or, if she had, would have called a pal to pull some strings. Carmen would have sought out an Alcoholics Anonymous meeting with the secondary goal of getting massage clients. Gail would have analyzed it to death and put a plan in place with short- and long-term goals not to let it happen again.

When Otis started to sing "Ole Man Trouble," Par returned to her story. "I was scared when I got stopped, then a little relieved because it was Dee Dee. But I got sarcastic at one point, and she made it clear she had no great love for popular kids from high school."

"Well, she was one of those fringe kids," Carmen mumbled as she ate a corn chip stacked with guacamole.

"Yes. And those fringe kids can grow up to be anything. It's bad when they get into positions of power," Gail said.

"I should have been a better person in high school—friendlier, you know, to kids like Dee Dee," Par said.

"We all should have been. But that's impossible. To be a better person, you need more life under your belt," Pinky counseled.

"And Pete never told me about the choke hold they put on your arm. Dee Dee gripped my arm and pinched her fingers into that sensitive part just above your elbow." She had Carmen stand up, and she used the pressure-point control tactic to steer her around the aft cocktail table.

"Ow! Point made," Carmen pulled away from Par and rubbed her arm.

"What was Gilligan doing while you were being abused by Dee Dee?" Pinky asked.

"He was out of it, crumpled in the backseat."

"I'm sure he feels terrible. . . "

A rumble of thunder exploded, and raindrops began pelting the conversation. Gail pulled in the anchor. They all wrapped themselves in towels and crowded underneath the Bimini top. Carmen motored the raft back to her dock.

"Maybe Nick should have talked to Dee Dee. He wasn't in the popular group," Gail hollered above the downpour.

Pinky elbowed Gail. "Yeah, but if you badger cops, they usually come down even harder. In other words, Nick could have gotten thrown in jail, too."

"She let him walk home."

"Bitch," Gail said.

"Double bitch." Pinky linked arms with Gail.

"Let's not invite her to the reunion next year," Carmen recommended.

"No punishment there. She never comes," Pinky said.

"You didn't seem drunk to me. No wobbliness or slurred speech," Carmen said.

Par nodded. "I hate to say this, but you want to know what I did as they booked me?"

All three women stared wide-eyed at Par.

Par turned her head and watched the rain make temporary pinpricks on the surface of the lake. "I smiled for my mug shot."

"Oh dear," Pinky said.

Gail ducked her head, walked aft, and unwound the rope from its cleat.

Carmen focused on pulling close to the dock. "That is a little weird."

At the house, Carmen turned off the air-conditioning and opened windows to let in the storm's breezes. She uncovered the guest of honor's treat, spread out on a platter: Pringles, half of each one coated in dark chocolate. They gasped with glee and ate with delight. Pinky made a toast: "To our favorite crazy heroine, Isadora."

"To my favorite drama queen," Carmen said.

"To a legendary genius of dance," Par said.

Gail clinked her glass three times but did not offer a fourth toast.

They drank more wine.

Par told them about Tony's call, Joey's fight with Jason Huff, her relief that he was not coming home today, and her fear of his reaction to her.

"Joey will be forgiving. He's a good boy," Carmen said.

"What about Todd? Have you told him yet?" Pinky asked.

"No. I've already sent him an e-mail this week. You know his rules."

"Oh, now you like his one-e-mail-a-week rule." Pinky plucked the last chip.

"Well, why not? He's going to be judgmental anyway. You know how antidrinking he is." Par moved off the barstool. "At least Nick's drinking less. Todd will be happy about that."

"Really?" Carmen licked salt from a finger.

"Well, less frequently. He has a new hobby, and I haven't had a chance to tell you guys with all the golf practicing I've been doing." Par walked to the center of the opened French doors and looked out. "I guess you'd call it a hobby. He's helping Natalie Johnson, our neighbor, groom and train dogs." She breathed deeply of the fresh air, then sat down on the couch.

Gail swiveled to face Par. "Is that legal in your neighborhood?"

"No, we're not zoned for commercial stuff, but no one has turned her in, and people in the 'hood keep bringing their dogs to her."

"When did this start?" Pinky asked.

"About a month ago. He's not going to the bar after work as much. At least he's being productive, though Natalie's not paying him."

The three friends joined her in the living room.

"He's never had a hobby to replace the loss of his band, so I bet this is a good thing," Pinky said.

"Maybe so." Par remembered accompanying Nick to his gigs. She had found him ultrasexy performing '60s music onstage.

But his band members had all disappeared, except Dave, the lead guitar player, who was close to his twenty-fifth year as a meter reader and to a retirement home in Florida. Occasionally they'd get together for a jam session, but mostly they just drank beer and lamented over the loss of the others. Jimmie, on sax, had been imprisoned for having a meth lab in his garage. Kevin, the bass player, had moved his wife and five kids to Montana for a construction job. The lead singer, Angela, had been a blond girl with a friendly smile as wide as Janis Joplin's but a voice that came up short. She'd started to drink Wild Turkey with breakfast, lunch, and dinner and died on her fortieth birthday of a major stroke. Ginger and Allison, the two backup singers, had moved to Detroit and married jazz musicians. Joel, the keyboardist, had gotten lucky in LA, finding steady work in a nightclub (he returned to Jackson occasionally to show off his surfer's tan). The trumpet and trombone players, Mitch and Mack, had vanished in New Orleans.

"Why don't you get a dog, Par? It might be a great thing before you go empty nest, and it could bring you two closer together." Carmen spoke from experience.

"I can't. I'm not over Squeeze." She and Nick had rescued Squeeze, a border collie, from the pound the summer before Todd had started school and Joey had turned three. He had fit right in as the middle brother. Ten years later, one scorched August day, his heart had stopped.

"Jesus, Squeeze died five years ago. You take forever to get over a death," Gail said.

Pinky straightened her posture. She exuded bossiness. "Your

father's gone, Pete's gone, and Squeeze is gone. You've heard the line 'bad things come in threes'—it's time you got over those deaths."

"Grief honors the dead," Par said firmly, hoping to end the topic.

"Obsessive grief dishonors the living. You have to move on," Pinky said.

Silence.

"What is this, an intervention?"

More silence.

"Carmen hasn't moved on."

They stared at Par.

"Don't go there," Pinky warned.

"Well, why not? The dog tags are still out, the peace lilies scream *s-t-u-c-k*." She waved an arm in a sweeping motion to draw attention to the room. "She has more pictures up of Dean than her son." Par looked directly at Carmen. "Your clothes are from the '60s."

"Stop it!" Carmen yelled.

"So, don't just pick on me," Par said as she twisted a button.

"This isn't about me, Par," Carmen said in a quieter voice, as she fingered her hemp choker with a look of such sadness, Par felt small and mean.

Gail could not handle conflict and went to the bathroom.

Pinky took charge. "Enough. This is an Isadora Fest. No arguing allowed." She paused for effect. "You both have made some good points. Kiss and make up."

The last thing Par wanted to do was fight at a Fest. She hugged Carmen, and they whispered apologies. By the time Gail returned, she carefully said what everyone was thinking: "Can we have some fun?"

"Yes," they yelled in unison, for that was the protocol for Isadora Fests—talk about the pain, eat, drink, laugh, and, of course, dance.

Pinky set up the stereo with five CDs. They sang along with Aretha, Diana, Marvin, Gladys and her Pips. Gail had the worst voice and Carmen the best. They imitated the Temptations line dancing to "I Wish It Would Rain."

* * *

All danced out and starved, they sat at the country table, joined hands—as Carmen always made them do—and each gave thanks for something.

"Thanks for keeping me safe in my plane," Pinky said.

"Thank you, goddess, for my dear friends." Carmen always said this.

"Thanks for my summers off," Gail said.

"Thanks in advance for helping me win the tournament."

They broke the circle, and Pinky passed her platter of bruschetta with goat cheese and tapenade. Gail had made an avocado-and-mango salad. The main dish, Carmen's specialty, was manicotti stuffed with lots of crab, smothered in a white sauce from a recipe she kept secret.

There were a few no-nos for dinner with this group: Pinky refused to eat nuts in salads, Gail despised cilantro, Carmen was allergic to strawberries, and Par wouldn't eat a water chestnut if you paid her.

They ate with concentration, murmured compliments, barely sipped their wine, and helped themselves to seconds.

"Do you think the district will fire me?" Par asked as she ate the last bite of manicotti on her plate. Being a substitute teacher kept her connected to the kids. As a sub, she loved how her students ran up to her in the hall or outside at recess and hugged her or screeched for her attention. The older students gave her high-fives and told her she was the best teacher they'd ever had. Par wanted to be a sub forever.

"That's a possibility, but you need to fight the charge. Get it off your record," Gail said.

Pinky nodded as she forked a chunk of mango. "Call the lawyer Gail knows. He specializes in DUI cases."

"Larry Knight. He'll charge a lot, but he's good at finding loopholes," Gail said.

"The fact that you got slandered by the newspaper might be in your favor," Carmen said.

"I don't believe Dee Dee's comment about my being just over the limit. She barely looked at the tube I blew into."

"That's good. Tell it to the lawyer," Gail said.

"Let's have dessert," Carmen asserted.

Par placed both hands on her stomach and said, "Can we wait a while? My stomach needs to settle around that fabulous meal."

"It's chocolate mousse," Carmen said, with a lilt in her voice.

"Oh, perfect, but I vote to wait a bit, too," Pinky said.

"Ditto," Gail said.

"Oh, hell. All right," Carmen relented.

They cleared the table and sat back down.

"Scratch my back, would you?" Par asked Carmen.

"Sure."

"Closer to the shoulder blade. Mosquito bites."

"'Tis the season."

"More wine?" Gail asked.

Heads nodded, and Gail went for the bottle she brought. "Vouvray. For the French in all of us."

"Love it," Pinky held out her glass.

"I don't want this weekend to end," Carmen said. "Monday's the funeral for Dawn, my neighbor from Crescent Lane."

"I thought she was getting chemo," Par said.

"Nothing helps pancreatic cancer. I did some research on the Web, and most people with the diagnosis die within a year. It's one of those bad cancers. She's got three kids under ten."

"That is so sad," Gail said.

"It's terrible. You never know, do you?" Par asked.

"If I got a terminal illness, I'd buy cartons of Winston cigarettes and smoke them past the filter," Pinky said.

"You miss it that much?" asked Gail.

"Every day."

"We wouldn't let you smoke like that," Carmen said.

They had all quit smoking when Carmen had been diagnosed with breast cancer. She was past her critical five-year mark, but watching her hair fall out, shopping with her for wigs, seeing her lose weight and energy, and worrying with her every time she had a checkup was enough not to risk giving themselves cancer.

After a moment, Gail said, "That's an idea. Why not?"

"Right. I'd smoke so much. With my morning coffee, on all my breaks—if I'm still working—after every meal, and definitely after sex."

"Yeah, right, like you're getting any. Or if you are, you'd better tell us," Par said.

Pinky rolled her eyes.

"I don't know. I think it's hard to say what you'd do with a death sentence. Everyone I've known with cancer opted for treatment. I think the will to live rules. Remember Sonia Sellers? She had that five-star brain tumor that killed her in six weeks. Most of that time she was weak and nauseous from chemo, which might have prolonged her life for a few days," Par said.

"Let's toast to life and remember Isadora's quote," Pinky said, as she made a hand-off motion to Gail.

"People do not live nowadays. They get about ten percent out of life." Gail giggled. The Isadora Fest's indulgences had relaxed her.

"We do better than that . . . don't you think?" Carmen asked.

They clinked one another's wineglasses.

"News flash: I'm researching Botox injections," Pinky said.

Carmen gasped.

"I'd shoot it right here to smooth out my worry lines." She placed a fingertip between her eyes.

"Yeah, and on your job, they'd be back in a week. Save your money," Par said.

"Those worry lines are part of your distinctive personality. Don't change a thing," Gail said as she touched Pinky's shoulder.

"Like my unique punctuation?" Pinky fingered a mole on her right eyelid the size of a ladybug.

"Exactly," Gail said.

"What do you think about me cutting my hair short like Gail's?" Par asked. She bundled up her braid close to the nape of her neck for effect.

"Don't ruin one of your best features," Carmen said.

"I've been thinking about it a lot lately. How nice and easy it would be to care for."

"What's stopping you?" Gail asked.

"I like it long in the winter. Also, I have a stupid hundred-dollar bet with Joy—if one of us cuts her hair, the other cashes in."

"How is Joy?" Pinky asked.

"Still beautiful and rich. Nothing has changed."

"She's charmed, that girl is," Carmen said.

"What's the latest?" Gail asked.

"I think she quit set designing to focus on modeling. Mom's coming home tomorrow night, and I'm picking her up in Detroit. She'll give me the full update on Joy's life." Par poured herself more wine. "They always have a blast together."

"You're jealous," Gail said matter-of-factly.

"You need to stop competing with a sister named Joy," Pinky added.

"Potty break," Carmen said, and left the room. Pinky and Gail went off to the second bathroom.

"I'm staying put," Par said. She looked around at Carmen's nautical-themed accessories. Shells, driftwood, mermaid art, throw pillows with starfish and whales, lighthouse table lamps. She knew if she ever realized her dream of owning a lake cottage, she would have fun decorating it with similar decor. Par twisted off the button she had earlier started to torture. She made a fist around it and thought about Joy. Joy, who had been seasoned by worldwide traveling and big-city living. Joy, who mingled with celebrities, dabbled in drugs, sampled multiethnic lovers. Joy, who had stopped coloring her hair and was now making a mint as a model flaunting her long ash-gray hair as cool and trendy, viable and vital, for aging baby boomers insecure about their loss of sex appeal and diminished worth in a youth-obsessed culture. Millions of women aspired to Joy's look of confidence in a slim but not thin body and a face that showed wrinkles with an expression of delight. Par had none of those things going for her. She did have a four handicap, two healthy sons, and a husband. But these things did not compare with Adele's claim that Joy had a special grace about her, like snow falling at midnight.

All three friends returned at the same time.

Par resumed the conversation. "My sister's a snob. Thinks she's better than anyone in Jackson."

"Which is why she never visits," Carmen said.

"Yes, and it's fine with me. I don't like being in her six-foot shadow."

A jazz riff came out of Gail's phone. She went out to the deck to take the call.

"What do you think Adele's reaction to your arrest will be?" Carmen asked.

"When are you going to tell her?" Pinky asked.

Par answered Pinky first. "Not in the car driving on I-94, that's for sure. Probably after I get her home." Looking at Carmen, she said, "Mom will have a fit; I'll feel eight years old again and brace myself to hear her one and only discipline tactic."

"And that is?"

"She'll say, 'You're going to hell for that.'"

"Really?" Pinky stared wide-eyed at Par. "That's a hoot."

"It's not funny to me. Those words have proved more effective than any yelling, spanking, time-out, or grounding."

"Par, you're forty-six years old," Pinky said.

"You guys don't understand." Par flushed.

"I think everyone is a little afraid of their mother. I'm surprised you never shared this with us before," Carmen said.

"I hate to think about it. I never would say that to my kids, wouldn't want them to feel the same shame or fright."

"You're a good mom, Par," Carmen said.

"Adele will be powerfully mad that the paper publicized it. Ten-to-one she'll make a scene with the editor at their next Women's Club event," Gail said as she returned from the deck.

"You actually think she'll wait for the next women's event to complain about the Parker name being slandered?" Pinky asked. She waved Gail to sit next to her and asked her who was on the phone.

"Jesse. He couldn't find the remote."

"Men are so helpless without their women," Carmen said.

"Oh, he would have found it if Gail hadn't answered," Pinky said.

"Phone's off now," Gail said.

Par walked to the stereo and turned off Marvin's voice singing "Ain't No Mountain High Enough." The sudden quiet and Par's comments "Carmen, get the champagne—I'll do the dance now" launched the symbolic ritual they had established at the original Fest. There was something about Isadora's personal tragedies and obsessive quest for perfection in her art that made each woman feel fortunate that what brought them together today was not as bad as what Isadora experienced: losing her two children on the same day, years of America rejecting her art, repeatedly losing lovers, the highs of wealth and the lows of poverty, the suicide of her mad ex-husband, her bizarre death—convertible Bugatti, long scarf, rotating tire—in a strangled flash.

Par left the room to change her clothes. She prepared in her mind as she thought of how Vanessa Redgrave must have rehearsed to dance in the movie *Isadora*. Par had watched it a thousand times.

Carmen poured champagne into four flutes and set up the track for Chopin's "Funeral March." Pinky and Gail readied the great room by lighting votives and pushing all furniture toward the walls. They sat on floor cushions with a view toward the lake. The atmosphere was expectant for Par's healing dance.

The guest of honor returned barefoot and clad only in the knee-length tunic. Par swallowed half her champagne, as Isadora had before dancing onstage. She stepped into the music's beginning, somber notes, and she marched in place, arms swinging. She balled her hands into fists, then flashed her palms at her friends—opening and closing her hands and eyes to gather and release tension.

Par infused her dance with the emotions she had experienced in the past forty-eight hours. She sank to her knees, bent at the waist, grabbed the front hem of her tunic, and pulled it high to cover her face (shame); she collapsed her body flat to the floor (sorrow). With the low, rumbling notes, she stood up and shuffled her feet, then stomped in a circle (worry). More marching—heavy stomping around the room, arms stiff; a switch to high-stepping, cutting the air with karate chops (anger); quick, repetitive motions of raking in air, then pushing it outward (regret). She spread out her arms like a conductor's—moving with the tempo, up and down with the beats.

Upon the first notes of the calm interlude, her audience clapped demurely. The mood lightened. Par loved the attention. She sighed and made her wrists appear limp and moved her extended arms like branches in the wind. She smiled. Taking tiny steps, her feet ran in small circles with the fluttering high notes. Her circles became bigger, and she ran forward, then backward with hands at her sides. Like a figure skater in competition, Par covered the entire room.

Ending with bold marching music, she turned to face her friends, simulating piano playing of the gloomy low notes. Her eyes were closed, lips firm, wrists and knees locked. She turned to face the lake, knelt on the floor, sat on her heels, and gently waved her upper body from left to right, with hands and fingers reaching for the ceiling.

The music stopped.

Pinky grinned. "Delightful."

"Bravo," Carmen and Gail clapped.

"I'm not finished," Par admonished.

Carmen nudged Pinky with an elbow, and Pinky nudged Gail. The gesture silenced them.

Par bent forward at the waist, bringing torso to thighs, her arms outstretched and palms flat on the floor—the yogic *balasana*. Carmen, Pinky, and Gail copied her, moving into child's pose. Seconds later, Par rolled onto the floor and firmly said, "Done."

* * *

Carmen served the mousse, topped with whipped cream and shaved chocolate, in martini glasses.

Gail whistled. "Nice presentation."

"Thanks. I made a double batch."

They dipped spoons into their dessert and ate quietly.

Sipping coffee, Pinky asked Par, "How's Ms. Politically Correct and Joey? Is the flame still hot?"

"Oh, yeah. It's more serious than I ever thought it'd get."

"Details," Pinky demanded.

"They're talking about going to the same college. Joey said he'd wait out a year so they could be freshmen together."

"Waiting? Doing what?" Gail asked.

"Working with Nick. Saving his money."

Carmen added cream to her coffee. "What'd you say about that?"

"Well, we won't pay out-of-state tuition. I told him he should go to Michigan State, but P. C. wants to go to Columbia or NYU on scholarship. She's brainy and she has plans. Big plans."

"For example?" Gail asked.

"Early in the summer, she came over and Joey wasn't home. I sat with her by the pool. She doesn't swim." Par rolled her eyes.

"And?" Pinky placed her elbows on the table.

"We talked. Or, I should say, she talked—all about her goals in life. To maintain a 4.0 GPA in high school; to study journalism at a top school, where she'll write for the college newspaper; to intern at the *Detroit Free Press* the summer before graduation."

"A good Michigander," Gail said.

"Then she wants to live in Washington, DC, and work for the Post, covering the White House. The girl knows more about politics than I do."

"No stretch there. You're a nonthinking Republican," Carmen said.

Par shot her a look. "She wants to learn Spanish or Russian or Arabic in her spare time to snag a foreign assignment. Her altruistic goal is to make a big enough salary to send money home to her parents, whom she describes as 'the less fortunate.'"

"That girl has got it together," Pinky said.

"She sighs a lot. It's as if she's bored to death and noting each minute of every hour, every waking moment." Par twisted a middle button on her blouse.

"The poor girl, she's just biding her time until college, when the real livin' begins," Pinky said with a knowing smile.

Carmen pulled on Par's hand to get her to stop twisting yet another defenseless button. "Any goals connected to marrying Joey? Or having kids?"

"No." Par put more sugar in her coffee. "I can't see Joey living in DC or in a foreign country."

"Or you don't *want* to see it," Carmen said.

"She could be your 'smart' kid, Par. You always wanted a smart kid," Gail said.

"We all know Carmen has the smart kid."

Ethan Noble was at Harvard, studying for a PhD in bioengineering. Carmen rarely talked about having a brainiac for a son. Who could relate?

"I don't need another kid." Par tapped her spoon on the table for emphasis. "She reminds me of Joy, the way she has her future all laid out. There's no doubt in my mind that with her confidence, despite her humble beginnings, she will get the best education and the most exciting jobs. She'll turn my boy into a sophisticate who I won't even know." She waved the spoon around. "Frankly, I think she'd be a better match for Todd."

"Don't go there," Carmen said.

"Well, she loves the Discovery and History channels. Those were Todd's favorite shows. I think Joey is faking interest in them for her."

"It's puppy love. They may break up before Joey graduates," Pinky said.

"That's true. How many people do you know who stayed forever with their first love?" Gail asked.

They all looked at Carmen, who had done just that.

"Well, Carmen was a lot older when she met Blake. So, she doesn't count." Gail patted Carmen's hand and said, "Sorry."

"No problem. I know you guys are jealous of what Blake and I have." Big smile. "Remember what Isadora said about raising kids—'the finest inheritance you can give to a child is to allow it to make its own way, completely on its own feet.'"

They all looked at Par.

"Well, she was more well-adjusted than I."

"No way. Isadora Duncan was not well-adjusted. She was crazy," Gail said.

"I can't believe you remembered that quote," Pinky said to Carmen.

"It's been my mantra since Ethan started grad school and we stopped sending him checks."

Par remembered that quote, too. Deep down, she agreed with it, but she'd never realized how hard it would be.

Late in the evening, Pinky choreographed a line dance to "Stop! In the Name of Love." Carmen videotaped the show. Around midnight, she brought out a bag of marijuana, which she said was premium weed. They smoked, watched the video, almost died laughing, and had trouble keeping their eyes open when "My Girl" came on the stereo. Pinky looked at Gail and tipped her head toward the dance floor. They slow danced. Close. Unnaturally close. Par could feel the heat between them and poked Carmen, who had fallen asleep. At the end of the song, Gail and Pinky kissed. It was a Hollywood kiss. A soft, deliberate French kiss.

It wasn't an ending to the evening Par could ever have expected. Her thoughts grappled with facts. Gail was married. Pinky had been married to Nate. They were best friends. They were straight. That kiss was special.

She and Carmen twittered under the influence of pot, then shut their eyes so as not to be caught watching. Sleep came unnaturally quickly.

FRIENDSHIPS TESTED

At breakfast, with wind chimes the accompaniment to bird songs, the best friends sat around a picnic table on the deck. They wore sunglasses. They drank coffee, ate lemon-ginger scones, blueberry muffins, crisp bacon, and large red grapes. They overpolitely passed butter, honey, jam, cream, and sugar while dabbing napkins to lips.

Par tipped crumbs off her plate behind her back for the birds and broached the subject everyone was thinking about. "So, how was your night upstairs, you two?" She spoke the question in a quiet, nervous voice.

Gail and Pinky looked at each other and broke off bites from the scone they were sharing.

Par wished she hadn't brought the scones.

"Tell us what's going on, and give it to us straight," Carmen whispered.

"Pun not intended?" Pinky whispered.

"Oh, come on. You two aren't gay. You've never been inclined that way."

No response.

"Have you? I mean, I thought I knew you," Par stammered.

"What about Jesse?" Carmen asked.

"I don't know. His job has ruined him," Gail said.

Par could understand that.

"When Jesse retires next year, it will take him forever to recover from his jaded, negative view of people. That's what those convicts have done to him." Gail looked out at the lake, pushed her plate aside with the back of her hand.

Gail had moved to Denver after college graduation to work for Dun & Bradstreet. Par had missed her terribly. When Gail returned to Jackson for a two-week visit one Christmas, Par threw a party and introduced her to Jesse Black. Jesse was a giant of a man who had played football at Michigan State as a linebacker. He exuded sex appeal with his brawn, his square jaw, his long eyelashes shielding bottle-green eyes, and his soft, deep voice. At that time he was quick to laugh and had a little boy's gleam in his eyes. He was unemployed but set up for an interview to be a guard at the State Prison of Southern Michigan.

Jackson had always been dependent on the industry of transportation—railroads, then automobiles. But from the 1930s on, crime became important to its economy. The prison, the largest in the country at one time, was north of town, and one of the city's largest employers. It was a foreboding place that citizens of Jackson rarely spoke of, until a prison break united everyone in fear and vulnerability—doors were locked and triple-checked, ears tuned to every news update, guns loaded or baseball bats placed at bedsides, lights left on through the night—even though common sense screamed that the escaped convict would run as far away from Jackson as possible.

Jesse and Gail had clicked instantly. They dined together every night, always ending up at his downtown apartment. Their mad rush of lust caused Gail to quit her job at the end of the second week with a phone call. She had her belongings shipped to Jackson, became Mrs. Gail Whitman-Black that spring, was hired by Jackson Community College to teach. She was the first woman Par knew to hyphenate her name.

"Do you think he suspects anything?" Par asked.

"No. Jesse's obsession with fantasy baseball keeps him totally occupied and out of touch with what I'm doing." She stood up and placed a hand on Pinky's shoulder. "I have to go," she said.

"Well, what if he finds out?" Par pressed.

"I'd be a little scared if he found out. I've taken too many domestic-violence calls," Pinky said.

Gail pinched Pinky's arm and said, "Quit it. We're careful."

"How long has this been going on?" Carmen asked.

Pinky grabbed Gail's hand and said, "Sit down. We have to tell them now."

Par felt an energy surge from Gail. Her usual reserved demeanor turned tense and wild.

"No!" Gail shook her hand loose from Pinky's grip. "You can't order me around. I'm not one of your emergency callers." She looked up at the cloudless sky and raised her arms like a preacher. "What if Jesse finds out?" She looked down on Pinky and said, "He's not going to find out." Those were her last words on the subject. Her car's tires spit gravel as she drove away from the scene.

Pinky, left at the table, had to endure the inevitable questions.

"How did this happen?"

"Long story," Pinky said. She squashed crumbs of scone on her plate with the flat end of her fork.

"When did it start?"

"About three months ago." She licked her fork.

"How could you have kept this from us for so long?"

She placed the fork, tines down, in the middle of her plate and gave them both a look that said, *Give me a break—you know why.*

"Where's this thing between you two headed?"

"It's anybody's guess." She ran her fingers through her thick auburn hair. Twice.

"What's it going to do to our group?"

She stood up, then sat right back down. "Nothing. Our group stays the same." She sat on her hands. "It has to." She crossed her legs, uncrossed them, sat up straighter, looked out at the lake, placed her hands on the table—flat, then clenched into fists.

Vague and incomplete answers, unsatisfying to Par, but she didn't want to push for more details. Pinky was frazzled, which was a state Par had never seen her in.

Carmen picked up dishes and took them into the kitchen. Par slid her chair next to Pinky and put an arm around her shoulders. "Our group has already changed. You two have crossed the friendship line." Par felt a pang of jealousy she did not understand, and it made her uneasy. She quickly moved back to her original place. "Carmen and I are on the outside of what you two have."

"I'm scared. I love Gail. You know, like I love you and Carmen. But you're right. We *have* crossed the line." She looked down and started to cry.

"Oh dear," Carmen said when she returned with a pot of coffee. She went right back into the house and came out with a bottle of brandy. They drank the spiked coffee with no conversation.

The stimulation of alcohol and caffeine kicked sweat glands into gear. "God, it's hot," Carmen said. "We should take a swim."

Par wiped her forehead with a napkin. "I didn't bring a suit."

"Like that would stop you?" Pinky asked as she blew her nose into a napkin.

"It's broad daylight. And look at all the boats coming out."

Pinky scanned the lake, her eyes filled with tears. She put another napkin to her eyes and pressed hard. Then, in a quiet voice, she said, "Gail's not my first woman."

Par gulped air, which made a choking sound in her throat. "What?"

"Oh dear," Carmen said. She reached for the last piece of bacon and the last muffin. "You need to tell us everything now."

Pinky stared into her cup, rubbed a fingertip around its rim a few times. Her eyes were red rimmed, and the punctuation mole seemed to take over her swollen right eyelid. She looked at her hands folded on the table. "There's another dispatcher, Charlotte Prentice. She's a lesbian. We've been going to some women's bars in East Lansing and Ann Arbor."

Par's mouth fell open.

Pinky reached over and pushed Par's chin up with the back of her spoon. "Not attractive," she quipped, and smiled for the first time that morning.

Par took the spoon from her and fought an urge to throw it into the lake.

"At first it was just for something to do. I've been bored lately. Then, instead of drinking and observing, I started talking and dancing with other women while Charlotte played pool or played the field."

"Unbelievable," Par said, and shook her head.

"Then what?" Carmen asked.

"I went home with a few of them."

"A few of them?" Par asked.

Pinky poured more coffee into everyone's cups. "That brandy was a nice treat, but it is early." Her calm had returned.

"I don't get how you can just change like that," Par said in a tight voice.

"What's your therapist say?" Carmen asked.

"Haven't told her."

"Not good," Carmen and Par said at the same time.

Par was tempted and terrified to ask how it had started with Gail.

"Gail's the romantic. You're impulsive. Someone's going to get hurt," Carmen said.

"Maybe it's a phase," Par said.

They had experienced other phases. Par remembered the year when all her friends had kissed one another's husbands. They had been in their late twenties, at parties. Their inhibitions down, they had innocently fallen into the habit, and they'd thought it fun. By the end of that summer, she and Carmen had watched Pinky watch Gail and Nate Hill, Pinky's husband, kiss for longer than was friendly fun, and the kissing swaps had abruptly ended.

"Remember that movie *Personal Best*? Mariel Hemingway ended up going back to guys," Carmen said.

"Yes. It's called bisexuality," Pinky said.

"It's not right," Par said.

"Well, who's to say what's right? It doesn't feel wrong," Pinky said, her voice defiant. She poured a splash of brandy into her empty cup and drank it down. "I hate the way you're looking at me right now," she said to Par.

"Sorry." Par shook her head to change her face.

"Let's clear the table," Carmen said.

"And take a break from talking about it, okay?" Pinky said.

Par went quiet. She stacked dishes on the kitchen counter.

"Go home, Par. I'll load the dishwasher later," Carmen said.

"I'm going to call Gail. See you later, Par, and good luck tomorrow," Pinky said.

"Thanks."

Carmen looped her arm through Par's and walked her to the Tahoe. They hugged. "Don't worry about this."

"Isadora Fests usually clear my head of troubles. Not this one." Par pouted.

"Things are different now. I wish we hadn't smoked the weed." Carmen looked at the ground.

"Don't put any blame on yourself."

Carmen kicked some gravel. "Oh, all right. And you focus on your golf game, and when this week's over, we'll tackle what those two have done." She walked into the house.

Par sank into the seat of her car and absorbed the sultriness of the day until she could stand it no longer. Starting the car and blasting the air conditioner with windows down, she waited for coolness.

Wow. It's unbelievable. She shifted gears. Driving by Pinky's Cavalier, two wheels in a ravine, Par read her bumper sticker—PRACTICE RANDOM ACTS OF KINDNESS. She remembered Pinky's habit of putting coins into expired meters where cars were still parked, and had to smile.

The Tahoe's shocks did nothing to mitigate the bumps and dips of the unpaved and winding road leading out of Carmen's neighborhood. Questions and thoughts bounced around in Par's mind about her friends' coupling. How would what was happening with Pinky and Gail change their clique? Could Pinky's therapist help them change back? Par did not like her friends keeping this secret. It felt like rejection. She had no problem with gay people. Or did she?

In college, Par had known two lesbians on her golf team. She had liked Heidi Lewis and Patti Simonton but hadn't spent time with them outside of golf practice and tournaments. One slow afternoon in the dorm, Heidi asked her to go to a women's fast-pitch softball game—MSU versus the University of Michigan. Par went for something to do and found the pitching an awesome blend of strength and precision. Heidi told her that half the softball team was gay and the other half just didn't know it yet. Par now wondered if that prophecy came true.

She remembered her third graders taunting other kids by calling them gay. Most didn't know what the word meant, but they used it as a putdown.

She remembered the tragedy of Daniel Mason, a star quarterback at Lumen Christi, the Catholic high school in Jackson. Many people had expectations that he would follow Tony Dungy's path to the NFL and make Jackson proud. His senior year, he committed suicide. His note admitted his "sin" of homosexuality. The *Citizen Patriot* covered the story liberally. Many people wrote letters to the editor attesting to Daniel's good character and great potential. Half the writers called for acceptance and action to support gay kids in schools. The other half were judgmental, based on "words in the Bible." A few people came out: a retired high school history teacher, a bank vice president, a waitress, a sales rep for computer hardware, a cable TV installer. These letters caused more letters of outrage and acceptance—again, about half and half. The end result was positive. Schools educated counselors in ways to support gay students and enforced zero tolerance for gay bashing. Through this collective spirit, people hoped more kids would not be lost in the same way.

Par punched her radio to life and pushed the CD 1 button for Aretha. "Rescue Me," Par's on-again, off-again theme song, filled the car with its vibrant tempo. Driving down Probert Road, she saw Eddie Murphy (another one of Pinky's nicknames for Dr. Murphy) rubbing the Corvette's hood with a chamois.

She gunned the gas pedal and sped home.

Nick was making a ham sandwich at the kitchen counter. He glanced at her and said, "How are the Isahorribles?"

"Great, as usual," Par lied.

"Are you feeling better now?"

"Somewhat better." She looked in the refrigerator to avoid eye contact.

"Joy called. You need to check your e-mail."

Joy never called. She whipped around to look at him. "Is Mom all right?"

"Yeah, I asked. She said they'd be lunching in Malibu and shopping in Santa Monica the rest of the day. She said you need to check your e-mail." He spread Dijon onto both slices of rye bread.

"Oh, she did? Well, I'll check it when I'm good and ready."

Nick shrugged and cut his sandwich in half.

"Did you and Blake have a good time last night?" She leaned an elbow on the countertop and gave him her full attention.

"It was okay. He brought over barbecued ribs from AJ's. We drank a twelve-pack and talked about you girls." He licked pickle juice off his fingers.

"Really?" She considered telling him about Gail and Pinky, feeling a need to share this bombshell news with someone.

"No. He trounced me four out of seven games in Ping-Pong. We bitched about gas prices—$1.70 a gallon. Unbelievable. Oh, and I had to listen to the usual US postal stories. You know, vicious dogs, catalogs weighing him down, heat exhaustion."

"Yes, I've heard them, too."

"And private, you know, guy stuff."

Par decided to keep her story about Pinky and Gail private. She stroked the hollow at her throat and felt overwhelmed with confusion. "Thanks for having him over." She kissed him on the cheek and felt a strong desire to assert her heterosexuality right there, right away. She took his lunch plate from his hands and set it on the counter, drew him close, and kissed him fully on the lips.

He pulled off his khaki hat and backed away slightly. "What about that e-mail?"

"What about this?" she asked, as she moved her body against him.

THE MOTHER

After their short but lively romp in the kitchen nook, Par and Nick quickly moved apart, pulling on shirts and zipping up shorts.

"Like old times, huh?" Nick said.

"Hmm, kind of." Par looked around the kitchen. "Where's the newspaper? I need to see who I'm paired with tomorrow."

"Front porch. I didn't bring it in." Nick picked up his plate again and tucked a *Rolling Stone* magazine under his arm. As he pushed open the screen door to the pool patio, he said, "After lunch I'm going next door to help groom two glam standard poodles."

Par frowned as the door slammed shut. She started to twist a button and went for the newspaper. Opening the sports section on her butcher-block island, she read the pairings and tee times on the last page. Naomi Chang, the tournament chair and a first-flight player, had paired her with Liz Carlton and Heather Lane. They were the second threesome teeing off at 7:40 am. Not exactly the playing partners Par would have picked, though she had developed a close summer friendship with Liz over the past several years. On qualifying day, Par liked playing with calm golfers, like Georgia Davis and Joyce Fitzgerald. Liz was forty-five, an Amy Alcott look-alike, a long-ball hitter who had trouble with an unpredictable hook. She had nervous habits that presented themselves as soon as she had a bad hole. The most annoying to Par was a loud sucking sound as if she was trying to get food out of her two front teeth while stroking a putt.

Heather Lane was a case. Par felt restrained respect for her. Heather had grown up with a father who was a chronic gambler and now resided in the State Prison of Southern Michigan for holding up a bank on Jackson's south side, and a mother who was a social outcast because she suffered from Tourette's syndrome and took her medicine irregularly. Heather Lane had an impressive golf reputation earned at the University of Florida in the mid-'90s. When Heather had returned to Jackson after graduation, she had married a successful real estate agent and given up the possibility of playing on the LPGA tour.

What Par didn't respect about Heather Lane was that she cheated. Yes, in the gentlemen's game of golf, where players often called penalties on themselves whether anyone saw the infraction or not, Heather did not count all her strokes. Par knew it, and everyone who had ever played with her in Jackson County knew it. No one knew for sure if this had been part of her game in Florida.

After Par felt she had ignored Joy's e-mail long enough, she went into her trophy room. At her computer table, she twisted a button and looked at the pictures of Isadora on the wall nearest her.

In four frames of consecutive dance moves, Isadora gamboled on a beach, exuding grace in a sleeveless, knee-length tunic. Her neck and arms seemed without bones; hands and fingers floated puppetlike. An eight-by-ten picture showed Isadora in a supple variant of the yogic spinal twist. It displayed fleshy thighs, an outstretched arm, palm open, as if making an offering or beckoning. The pose enticed Par to twist her back once left, once right. She heard a crack on each side and felt more relaxed.

Then she read the e-mail:

Sit down and hold on for this e-ticket news! Our mother spotted an old boyfriend (not old, really—ten years younger than Adele) at a café in Santa Barbara. His name's Norman. Didn't she name her cats Norman? And he's cute—well, not cute, really, but attractive in that way successful men in their fifties are. He's loaded, not loaded like drunk, but loaded with money from a chain of specialty-cheese stores that line cities on the East Coast, and he's thinking about expanding to my West Coast! His wife (third wife) died four years ago. You should have seen him light up when he saw our mother. If only I could have a man look at me like that! But this isn't about me, now, is it?

Par let out a low moan.

Mom's in a salon right now, getting her hair cut—yes I said cut—and it's going to be short. Like Winona Ryder's. I'll send pictures. She's not returning to Detroit tonight. Don't worry, I'll watch them as closely as I can, at least when they aren't holed up in his ocean-view suite at the Loews hotel.

Par looked at Isadora again, crossed her arms to contain the shock, willed herself to keep reading.

She was afraid to call you and said you wouldn't understand, and she worried that you'd feel she wasn't interested in your golf week, but she is—it's just that she loves this guy. Par, she really loves him! I can tell by the way she looks at him, and he feels the same way. Weird, isn't it, that Mom's having sex with a guy we don't know? Or weird that, at sixty-eight, she's even having sex? She's going to stay out here at least for the duration of Norman's business trip, which ends August 8. Can you stand taking care of her cats for another three weeks? Of course you can. What choice do you have, really? Wish I could help you out. No, that's a lie and you know it.

Ciao,

Joy

PS: I'm hoping Adele doesn't move out here. That would cramp my style, and at my age I need all the style I can get.

Par shut her eyes tight, smelled sex. She wondered, *How long has it been? Too long.* She spoke to the computer screen: "Norman, a man in Adele's life. That was her secret." She twisted a button off, placed it in the ceramic dish that held paper clips, and typed one sentence in reply:

Who's going to take care of your mother's cats while I'm at Mackinac Island next week?

Par

She clicked Send.

A Parker-Swink ritual was to spend the week after Par's big golf tournament with the family on Mackinac Island. That was her way to reconnect with her boys and her husband, her offering of appeasement for neglecting them during golf season.

As she reread the e-mail, her emotions snagged on the words: *old boyfriend, expanding to my West Coast, hair cut, not returning, watch them, afraid to call, loves him, August 8, cramp my style.*

Once again, her mother and Joy were sharing, and Par was excluded.

She went to the pantry for Pringles. At the window seat, she munched and watched two blue jays eat lunch at a bird feeder.

Where the hell did Norman come from? Where and when had Adele met him? College? Before or after she married Henry? Ten years younger would make him fifty-eight. He was only twelve years older than Par and ten years older than Joy! Had he been a high school boyfriend? Was he a Jackson guy? Had Par ever met him? Had Adele met him at a Republican convention?

She did the math on a grocery-list notepad. Adele had had Joy at twenty, Par at twenty-two, had been married to Henry from 1952 to 1978, then widowed at forty-six, the same age Par was now. She must have known him after Henry died. There had been twenty-two years when it could have happened. Why the secret? Or had she had an affair with him while married?

Placing her elbows on the table, Par drummed her fingertips on its surface. "Oh my gosh, they've got the lust thing going," she said.

Pete Masterson had brought high lust back into Par's life. The first time, though, had been in high school, senior year, when Allen Gaines had caught her attention. Allen was tall, dark-skinned, and soft-spoken, a talented artist and well-documented ladies' man at seventeen. Par felt on fire when he talked to her. They started meeting after school and walking at Ella Sharp Park. He drove a maroon Le Sabre, and their make-out sessions became all Par could think about. Allen had condoms in his glove compartment, and he'd remind her of them, but he never pushed. These new sensations and the taboo of dating a black man came to an abrupt end when her father found out Allen was the guy who had asked her to the prom.

Par's mother had told Henry about Allen after meeting him for the first time. Allen had asked her permission to keep Par out on prom night until one AM because of a midnight feast at Carmen's. Adele had said, "I'll speak to her father about it."

Par remembered sitting in a beanbag chair in the basement, talking on the phone to a friend about dresses and jewelry for the dance, when she heard Henry scream, "No!" He came downstairs and grabbed Par out of the chair, threw the phone down, and shook her while yelling never to go out with black boys or he'd disown her and she'd be on the street with one suitcase and he'd change all the locks and forget he'd ever had a second daughter. His fingers left bruises that lasted a week on her upper arms and remained on her nerves forever.

Because she had never felt that high lust with Nick or her short-term college lovers, she had thought it was a once-in-a-lifetime allowance. When she'd felt it with Pete, she'd realized it was taboo that created the intensity, and she had enjoyed its return.

"Hey, Mom."

Par jumped. She hadn't heard Joey come in. He stood at the butcher-block island with his hands clasped on its top. She went to him.

He put his head down.

She tilted up his chin gently with two fingers. "Let me see, dumplin'."

He took a step back, stood up straight. His energy filled the room. "Mom, don't call me dumplin'. I'm not a little kid."

Par felt slapped in the face. "Oh, right. You got the virgin fight out of the way, and now you're a . . . what . . . a man?"

He glared at her.

She stared back, felt her grip of him slipping. His bottom lip was puffed to twice its normal size. It had a vertical scab at its center that had just split open. She grabbed a sheet of paper towel, ran it under cold water, and offered it to him.

He licked away the fresh blood and pulled in his lip, guarding it with his front teeth.

"Here." She handed him the drippy towel. "You might need it later."

His right cheekbone was swollen and smudged violet. He hadn't shaved, and he looked much older than seventeen. "Okay, I won't mother you right now." She hoped that was the right thing to say. "Are you hungry? Want a bacon sandwich? String cheese?" No response. "Thirsty? I bought you Cherry Cokes."

"No, thanks." He rubbed his chin stubble. "Are you all right?"

"Yes. I'm sorry you had to defend me with your friends at camp. Friday night was the worst night of my life." She didn't know how much to say. "Not a very good example, am I?"

"Well, it's done. Nothing you can do now."

"You're so practical." She wanted a hug but held back. She wanted to tell him about Adele but held that back, too.

"I'm going over to P. C.'s."

When had his voice turned into Nick's?

He turned away slowly, as if there was more to say, or maybe he did want some mothering.

"Maybe you'll want to shave first?" She liked her boys clean-shaven.

He stopped.

She flinched, knowing she had said the wrong thing—again.

"No, I don't." He walked away and grabbed his car keys off the hook by the door.

Maybe his girl will put him in a better mood, she thought, and felt comforted by the fact that, with his lip wound, they wouldn't be making out for a while.

Par went to the pool, stripped, and swam laps. At each flip turn, she pushed hard away from the pool's wall and tried to push away thoughts of her mother and the amorphous Norman. Since her father's death, Par had appreciated her mother's not having replaced him. As a widow, Adele refused to date any of the men who called or rang the doorbell. She often said, "Married to the best makes a second man a pest."

Par wondered how Adele could have changed her mind and worried she would leave Jackson to live with the cheese man. After many laps, she stopped in the shallow end and saw Nick staring at her from a lawn chair.

"You won't believe it." She heaved from the effort.

"What gave you that energy rush?" He got out of the chair.

"My mother has a boyfriend." She dunked the back of her head into the water to get all the hair off her face.

Nick placed his magazine on the patio floor, walked over to Par, and crouched in front of her at the shallow end of the pool. "What are you talking about?"

"She's not coming home tonight. Joy's e-mail said that she ran into an old boyfriend and now they're holed up in his hotel room." She yelped and swam another lap.

On her return to the shallow end, Nick grabbed her wrist. "Par. Your mother, with a boyfriend? What's going on?"

Par told him the whole story.

"Wow, that's weird. Who'd a thought?" he said.

"Not me. Not in a million years." She swam some more. She thought about how Henry's murder had affected Adele. Overtaken with manic energy, she had shocked Par by spending long days with Buddy Oscar, immersing herself in the details of running the Chevrolet dealership. Buddy had no choice but to let her be his shadow and share his knowledge. She even slept at the dealership—in one of the glistening new cars in the showroom. As undignified as that was, she justified it simply as not wanting to miss anything. She developed an obsessive focus on the financial statements, that being an area she had some confidence in, having studied bookkeeping before marrying. Adele's transformation from homemaker to dealership owner was swift. She became Par's father, without the practical jokes.

MASSAGE THERAPY

Swimming had not soothed Par as much as she'd needed it to. The golf tournament was tomorrow. Her neck and shoulder tendons felt pinched. She swallowed a handful of aspirin and called Carmen from the cabana. As soon as Par heard her friend's voice, she blurted, "I'm having a nervous breakdown. Can you help me?"

"What happened?"

"Joey hates me. My mother is sleeping with some guy named Norman in LA." She gulped air as tears streaked her face. Her hands shook.

"Oh, honey. Come on over. We'll talk, I'll give you a massage, and we'll have some pie."

"Pie?" Par sniffled.

"You bet. Apple. It just came out of the oven. Special request from Blake."

"You're such a good wife. Much better than I am."

"Don't leave us alone with this pie for long."

"On my way."

Par told Nick he was on his own for dinner. She drove quickly to Carmen's, let herself in, and nodded to Blake, sitting at the country table with fork in hand, two bites of pie left on his plate, and the Sunday *Detroit Times'* sports section splayed open.

"How's the pie?" she asked.

"Exceptional. Good luck tomorrow."

"Thanks, dear." She walked upstairs, wondering how much Carmen had told him about the previous night and the juicy gossip about her mother.

At the top of the stairs, Par stopped and breathed in the scent of lavender candles. Blake had converted the loft into a massage room. A massage table sat in the center; shelves along two walls were stacked with a variety of essential oils and lotions; books on anatomy, reflexology, aromatherapy, erotic massage; CDs for meditation; and polished Petoskey stones. A poster showed chakra-energy and muscular systems. Blake had installed gliding windows for an expansive view of the lake.

Carmen came up behind her, and Par twitched. "Jumpy, aren't you?"

"I'm a wreck."

"Oh, I doubt that," Carmen said, as she patted the table. "I put on your favorite sheets": multicolored hot-air balloons scattered on a pink cotton fabric.

"Nice." Par left her undies on and lay down on the massage table. A small fan stirred the air, giving no relief from the heat. "I wish you'd put AC in here."

"No way. I hate artificial coolness. It's good for you to sweat, and your muscles are more supple and responsive when they're warm."

"If you say so. My neck is stiff, and I have a monster headache."

"I'll start at your feet. Everything is connected to these size eights."

Par repeated Joy's news about her mom. The telling of it helped ease some of the shock. Carmen's touch and the Celtic harp music combined to place Par in a state of deep relaxation. She hoped to retain some of this feeling for the next day's round of golf.

Halfway through the massage, Carmen said, "Don't get mad, but I'm happy for your mom. I think it's hard to realize and accept that mothers have full lives, identities separate from being a parent. Kids rarely think about that."

Par tensed the thigh muscle Carmen was kneading.

"Let it go, Par. It couldn't have been easy for Adele to have Joy send you that e-mail." Carmen placed thumbs at the top of one knee and slid them around to the bottom of the kneecap, then back to the top. She did this several times to both knees.

"I always wanted to be close to my mom." Par's sadness surfaced in tears.

Carmen handed her a tissue.

"I hope she'll believe me when I tell her Dee Dee had it in for me."

"You two can rally around your fight against the charge. And you have to support her relationship with Norman."

"Ugh."

"Very caring." Carmen squeezed each toe.

Par smiled.

"Turn over. I want to get at your hamstrings and back."

Par rolled onto her stomach and fidgeted until her face was

comfortable in the cradle. Carmen tucked the top sheet to the inside of her right leg. "Wow, more mosquito bites. They love you."

"At least somebody does."

"I'll give you some tea tree oil to stop the itching, and the smell will deter the buggers from biting again."

"The smell?"

"It's not so bad. Trust me." Carmen continued the massage.

"Why is everyone changing now?" Par asked.

"Bad timing, isn't it? Your golf week and all."

"You got that right."

Carmen kneaded the back muscles, and with thumbs massaged the spinal column and shoulder blades. Par felt the muscles loosen and knew it would be good for her game tomorrow.

"How do you think this thing between Pinky and Gail will end up?" Par asked.

"Who knows? Did you ever expect something like this could happen?"

"Never."

"If they stay together, won't it be awkward?"

"It sure felt weird this morning."

"If they break up, won't there be bad feelings?"

"There are always bad feelings after a breakup." Par thought back to watching Pinky and Gail in their slow dance. That was some kiss. The type of kiss that Nick no longer bothered with, the type of kiss Par longed for. "Does Blake kiss you like they kissed?"

"Sometimes. Usually the pot makes him slow down and everything's better."

"This may sound terrible, but it seems like incest to me," Par said.

Carmen began a scalp massage. Very quietly and thoughtfully, she said, "I see what you mean. We're like sisters."

"Closer than most sisters, I think."

"Yes. I'd like it to stop. But let's not talk about them right now. You're in crisis overload, and we have a lifetime to figure out their situation."

"As long as Jesse doesn't find out."

"It's out of our control." Carmen gently tugged Par's hair, pinched her earlobes, and said, "You're done, my friend, unless you feel any tight spots."

Par stretched. "No, that was great."

"Okay, don't rush getting up. I'll be downstairs."

Par stayed put several minutes to enjoy how her body felt.

She slipped grudgingly off the table, and as she dressed, she noticed ashy stubs of incense in a round pewter ashtray, HEALTH, LOVE, WEALTH, AND TIME TO ENJOY THEM printed around its flat rim—a wedding present from Par and Nick. An ironic message for smokers. Par was glad Carmen had found a new use for the gift and hadn't sold it for ten cents at a garage sale.

* * *

On the deck, Carmen served chamomile-mint iced tea. They ate generous slices of pie. It was a perfect summer evening—eighty degrees, a slight breeze, low humidity. A few rafts and sailboats drifted on the lake.

"Remember when my dad died?" Carmen asked.

"Yes. I remember you two weren't very close. I never understood that."

"Well, he was prickly. Not at all like your father. Anyway, Mom started doing everything with her gal pals, women she had completely lost touch with because Dad wanted her all to himself. She took up old hobbies I never knew she'd had—playing the violin, making jewelry, painting abstract art."

"She went out a lot, too."

"Oh, she became a lot more interesting. Wednesday nights became movie nights. Friday nights, she went to the Detroit symphony. Sunday was her grieving day for Dad and Dean. She'd cook macaroni and cheese and barbecued ribs—their favorite foods. Sunday evenings, she looked through picture albums with a box of Kleenex at her side."

"But not anymore."

"Right. With Alzheimer's, she doesn't remember a thing about the men she lost."

"Maybe that's a good way to end up," Par said carefully.

"Now *I* cook macaroni and cheese with ribs on Sundays."

Par smiled, and Carmen looked wistful.

"Another piece of pie?"

"A sliver. You make the best pie."

"And like you with golf, I love to practice."

* * *

At times, walking into her childhood home reminded Par of the bond between her sister and mother and the bond she had had with her father—the former still vibrant, the latter extinct. Pairings like this were natural in families, often immutable and always dysfunctional.

Par fed and petted the Normans but refused to speak their name.

In the kitchen, she listened to the first of two messages on her cell: "It's Jule Gladstone. I am incredibly sorry about that article in Friday's paper. Call me."

Par tapped in Jule's number and leaned against the counter.

"Hello, Ms. Parker."

"Who put it in?" Par walked out to the deck.

"That question is at the top of my to-do list. Rest assured, I will rustle the rat out of his or her hole and make sure that person never works in the newspaper business again."

She sounded out of breath. Worked up about this egregious error. Par didn't know what to say.

"Is your mother around?"

"No. She's in California, and at this point her return date is unknown."

"Good. I'll write a letter of apology to you and publish it tomorrow. The city needs to know our protocol was breached and I'm accepting responsibility. No one who's arrested for driving under the influence gets a splashy write-up unless there's a collision and people are hurt or killed. Innocent until proven guilty and all that. Do you think it will help?"

"Jule, the damage has been done." Par twisted a button. "You know that."

"Were you driving impaired?"

"No. The deputy who stopped me was a high school nobody, and she took pleasure in abusing me. I'm calling a lawyer."

"Call Larry Knight. I've heard he's the best."

"A friend already recommended him, so thanks for confirming he's the right guy."

"Good. Just know I'm mad as a hot poker and the culprit is going to feel it pierce his pea head."

"Don't you mean pea brain?"

"Whatever. You call Larry and use my name if you want."

"I will. You owe me."

"Yes, I do."

The second message was from Buddy Oscar. He cussed out the newspaper and said he didn't believe a word of it. Par liked Buddy. He had endured as sales manager of the Chevy dealership through two owners after her father. She liked the contrasts in the way he looked. He had lots of wiry hair on the sides of his head and baldness on top that made him look clownish until you noticed his bushy eyebrows and serious eyes nesting underneath, lips thin and firm like a closed lid. He rarely laughed, loved to read motivational books about the "art" of selling, and was a huge fan of the all-time positive thinker, Dr. Norman Vincent Peale.

Twenty years ago, Par had been playing golf with Georgia Davis, Rhonda Stein, and Liz Carlton. One last round in Jackson with her favorite threesome before heading off to LPGA Qualifying School. It hadn't been a great round, but she had just made two birdies in a row, had just walked up to the tee box on seventeen, when she saw a man in a golf cart driving up the middle of the fairway. It was such a queer sight that the four golfers laughed and waited for the driver to move away from the fairway. As the cart came closer, Par recognized the driver. It was Buddy Oscar. She knew something must be terribly wrong for him to be away from the dealership in the middle of the day, and odder still for him to be on the golf course. He drove the cart onto the tee box, which was something a golfer knew not to do, for it was sacred ground and you didn't want to damage the grass with the weight of the cart.

Stepping back, away from the cart, Par felt the spikes on her golf shoes scrape the grass. Buddy's eyes were red from crying. He shook his head, patted the seat. She looked at her friends, who looked serious and confused. No one spoke. Buddy's face turned into a grimace, and he said, "There's been a shooting." He glanced at her friends, took a deep breath, then pushed out the words at Par: "Your father's been killed."

Par went deaf. She watched Georgia strap her golf bag and pull cart into the back of the electric cart. Liz led her by the arm to the passenger's seat and made her sit down. Her body moved stiffly, as if her joints had frozen. Buddy drove fast toward the parking lot, and Par felt the hot air spread her streams of tears. He drove her home in his black '61 Impala. She found her mother in the library, sitting in a wingback chair. On the burgundy carpet, Adele had dropped or tossed many wadded tissues. Par had never seen her mother cry, had never seen her make such a mess. Adele stood up and grabbed Par in a hug of strength and need. It knocked the wind out of Par. She still couldn't hear. Par pushed her mother away because she needed space to breathe. She ran down to the basement and screamed. Midscream, her hearing came back. She ran back upstairs to be with her mother, but it was too late. Adele was on the phone with Joy.

* * *

Adele's grandfather clock bonged eight times. Par wanted a night swim and to be in bed by ten. She slapped a mosquito away from her arm and walked back into the house.

Upstairs, she stopped in front of the gilded mirror at the end of the hallway in the wing with the guest bedrooms. She stood really close. For forty-six years old, she thought she was holding up pretty well. Her eyebrows were plucked in a style that Joy had taught her that added roundness to her eyes. She looked critically at the two scratches of wrinkles under each eye—like an accountant's symbol for a final total. Par knew that wouldn't be the final number of wrinkles. With her fingertips, she spread the skin upward and absorbed the momentary pleasure of looking like a twentysomething again.

"That's not real," she said, and let her hands drop to her sides. She walked through her parents' spacious bedroom, peeked into the large walk-in closet, and regretted her voyeurism the moment she saw her father's section—a huge empty space—then went into their bathroom. The bidet next to the toilet had been the talk of Adele's Women's Club after her parents had remodeled. Par smiled and sat on the edge of the Jacuzzi.

Avoiding going home and needing to be in motion, Par went back into their bedroom, which was full of mission-style furniture. A green-and-beige quilted bedspread draped the king-size bed; the thick brown carpeting had faded and flattened where her mother tracked daily.

Par sat on the bed, opened her mother's drawer of the nightstand. Her heart beat fast. She knew this drawer was not her business. Rifling through the items, her fingers touched Adele's hairbrush, tube of hand lotion, pens with hotel logos, presidential-hopeful buttons, hankies with the embroidered initials AMP, an ancient *Automotive News*, spearmint Tic Tacs, and the Sacred Hearts' scapular. The red-and-white scapular of Par's youth! She quickly pulled it out and scattered the clutter until she found the two others.

She looked around the room, as if expecting to be discovered. Why had her mother saved them? She squeezed all three in her hands and shook her head, not knowing the answer.

Par slipped the scapular around her neck, touched the felt, and tucked it under her shirt. There. That felt right.

QUALIFYING DAY

Six AM, qualifying day. Par would be going after good press—bold headlines—to shroud everyone's memory of the DUI article. Deciding to skip her morning swim to get to the course early to practice, she loosely braided her hair, sprinkled some talcum powder underneath her sports bra, and dressed in a turquoise linen camp shirt and white shorts. The radio reported it was going to be in the midnineties, with humidity to match. She stuffed a water bottle with ice and put it and an extra towel in the long pocket of her golf bag.

Par turned on the air-conditioning and went into her trophy room to psych herself up for the competition. She touched the picture of her and Rosie Jones at the US Women's Open. Rosie had autographed a scorecard for Par that Par now pulled out of a mail slot on her desk. She absorbed what Rosie had written above her signature: *Relax and attack*—her competitive mantra.

She sat down. Thoughts of her mother and Norman dominated her mind. She was upset that her mother hadn't delivered the news herself, angry that she wouldn't be around for Par's golf week, worried that she was with a man Par did not know, hurt that she had kept this secret from her, and nervous about how this news might change their future.

Relax and attack.

She borrowed from Pinky's therapist's advice and visualized placing her negative thoughts and worried feelings into an imaginary box, sealing it with tape, and placing the box in her closet. She needed to concentrate on golf. Today was about birdies and pars, not Adele and Norman, not Gail and Pinky, and not Joey.

Relax and attack.

Par looked at the picture of Isadora, dressed, as usual, in a free-flowing tunic, strolling a tree-lined dirt path, her arms raised, exalting life. "Maybe I'll feel that good about my round today," she said.

On the kitchen counter, she read a good-luck note from Nick. The PS said Joey was working with him, which seemed odd because Joey loved to sleep in late during the summer. *Well, everyone else is changing—why not him?* she thought.

Breakfast was a toasted English muffin with blackberry jam on one side and thin slices of Gruyère on the other. She ate it as a sandwich while driving to the golf course. She had one clear advantage for qualifying day: the tournament was at her home course—a course she played weekly, a course on which she knew what club to hit from every lie, every angle, and from any distance to any green. For the past thirty years, she had shot in the seventies or low eighties to make the cut for the championship flight. Every year, though, with a golfer's fragile confidence, Par worried that she'd bomb on

Q-day and have too many errant drives, putts rimming the cup, chips running long, sand shots staying in the sand (sins to a golfer), and end up in the first flight, suffering unspeakable pain to her ego.

She parked under the branches of a mammoth elm tree that offered the one spot of shade in the half-acre lot. Her reward for getting there early. She snapped off the air-conditioning and saw Connie Lyons zoom into the lot in her baby-blue Mercedes SL coupe, saw her fishtail on the gravel, then lost sight of her in the dust cloud, until the dust settled and she saw the Mercedes parked at an angle next to her Tahoe.

The Honorable Judge Walter Lyons, Connie's husband, would have had a stroke if he'd seen this crisp piece of driving.

They both got out of their cars.

Par wasn't ready to look directly at Connie. Instead, she looked at her golf outfit: pale-blue Bermuda shorts with a crease ironed down the middle, a white sleeveless polo shirt. Of course she wore matching Callaway golf shoes.

When she did look at Connie's face, she saw a look of sympathy and felt embarrassed.

"Hi, Par," Connie said in a cheery voice.

They hugged briefly.

"What do you have in you today?" Connie asked.

"Seventy-five, I think." Par looked up at the sky and said, "No, I hope."

"I hear there's a new girl moved here from Muskegon. Kim Allen. You may need an under-par round to be medalist today. She's a scratch player."

"Lots on my mind, you know."

"Forget it for this week." Connie opened her trunk and pulled out a bright-green-and-white golf bag. Dalmatian heads covered each of her woods. "By the way, Walt thought that article and picture were unfair."

"Thanks. I did, too. I don't think I was over the limit, like the deputy said."

No comment from the judge's wife.

Par squeezed out a blob of sunblock onto her palm and spread it on her arms and legs. "How about you? Is this your week to break eighty?"

"Ha! I'd trip out of my mind if that happened."

* * *

After Par paid her greens fees in the clubhouse, Naomi Chang pulled her aside and bought her coffee. Par thought she was going to mention the article and arrest, but instead she asked, "Will you keep an eye on Heather today?"

"What do you mean?" Par played dumb. She sipped the coffee.

"Help her count her strokes, Par. It will be to your benefit."

"Naomi, when I compete, I pay attention to my swing, the conditions, the pin placements, and positive self-talk. I'm not going to pay attention to counting Heather's strokes. It's too distracting for me. And besides, I've got my own troubles." She leaned in toward Naomi with the last sentence.

"I know. I read about it." She patted Par's shoulder. "Start taking cabs. Everyone stays safe that way."

Par bristled. "Thanks for the coffee. I have to get to the putting green."

"Listen." Naomi squeezed Par's arm. "Please reconsider. I told the board that I'd call her on cheating this year to put an end to it. They agreed that there's been too much whispering behind her back for us to continue to do nothing."

Par sipped more coffee and said nothing.

"But we can't do anything after the fact, or if no one will address it as it happens."

"Send a scorer out with us, like the pros. I'm not going to get involved in this crusade. She's way bigger than I am, and I don't want a seven-iron implanted in my forehead. I just want to play."

They both laughed at what they hoped was an exaggeration of what Heather Lane would do if accused of cheating.

Par poured out the half-full cup of coffee in the restroom's sink. The caffeine had sharpened her nerves to a fine, pointy prick. She soaked a small towel under the faucet for cleaning her clubs after each shot. Two dry towels were hooked to her bag to wipe off the sweat from her hands and face. With thirty minutes before her tee time and feeling edgy, Par went to the practice putting green. There was only one woman already practicing at the south end of the green. Kelly Hayes, twenty-two years old, a natural blond, with a short, compact build, had a penchant for golf shirts with vertical stripes and skorts. She had made it to the semifinal round the year before and had been beaten by Rhonda Stein, fifty-five years old, a bleached blond with a custom-made set of clubs, including more woods than irons, which helped her maintain distance and accuracy as she aged. If Kelly ever became a really good putter, Par knew she'd dominate the match-play tournament.

Setting up at the opposite end of the green, Par practiced with a specific routine to build confidence for the short and long putts to come. She dropped three golf balls a foot away from a cup. She tapped each one firmly into the hole. She did that two more times, then placed the balls a little farther away from the cup. When she gradually moved to twenty feet away, she stroked a few to get a feel for the long putts.

After Par had sunk several six-footers and started to move back to around eight feet, she looked around to see who else had arrived. At one edge of the green, she saw a stranger in black shorts and a red polo shirt—tall, slim, darkly tanned, with perfectly etched calf muscles—bent slightly over an imaginary golf ball, swinging her putter back and forward, over and over, clearly locked in some kind of Zen mode of practice.

Must be the new girl, the scratch player. The one to beat.

The putting green started to get crowded. Georgia Davis, Rhonda Stein, and Joyce Fitzgerald, veteran golfers, came over to Par to see how she was doing and offered words of condolence, words similar to what they offered when she lost golf matches. She tried not to feel like a loser, though. She told them in a quiet voice that jail had been a nightmare, the article had made her feel humiliated, and she was glad to be at her favorite course, playing in her favorite tournament, but held back from saying she had to win this year, because they were more than friends—they were her competitors—and they all wanted the title one more time as badly as she did.

She appreciated these women. When she had first started to play in the women's tournaments, Par couldn't have understood how much a day on the golf course and a few drinks afterward, with laughter and conversation, meant to these women with children and husbands. On league and tournament days, their other roles as wives and mothers, teachers, nurses, lawyers, real estate agents, and daughters and siblings became background trivia. They focused on slow backswings, steadiness over putts. They focused on firm grips to hit out of sand or high rough, all with a keen concentration of the kind that precludes thoughts of past and future.

When Par became a wife with a full-time job and absorbed the drudgery of keeping a clean house, grocery shopping and cooking, bill paying, and loads of laundry, she was never able to stay on top of it. Household chores. Repetition extraordinaire. How quickly the bliss and ease of living that came with being dependent on parents dissolved with the marriage contract. Nick had been raised not to do anything around the house. *Laundry? What's that?* He knew only clean clothes folded neatly and placed in his drawers. Par remembered one time of rebellion when she had stuffed unpaired socks in his drawer. It had felt so good.

The younger championship-flight players either nodded hello to Par or ignored her. They might not have read the paper or simply didn't care to broach the subject. She noticed Hilary Harris, the defending champion, a senior at Western Michigan University, sitting on a bench by the green, with one arm stretched out on the top rail, legs crossed at the knee, a pose that hiked up her shorts enough to flash a very firm upper thigh that the sun never touched. She sipped a latte. She looked smug watching the players on the putting green. And why not? She was exempt from qualifying, so today's round was just for practice. Par remembered how it felt to be defending champ—coming out on qualifying day without a care in the world, already having earned a berth in the championship flight. Jealousy made Par's eyes squint, and her resolve to shoot a low round increased.

Par walked over to the ball washer and overheard Brooke Benson, a chatty twentysomething wearing bright-orange shorts and a turquoise T-shirt (the girl had no fashion sense), telling Kim Allen, the new girl, about the course.

"The front side is hilly and long and starts with two par fives."

"That's okay. I hit it long."

"Did you know this course was rated by *Golf* magazine as one of the top one hundred public golf courses in the country?"

"No. I don't read golf magazines. What's the back nine like?"

"Lots of water. I mean *lots.* A meandering lagoon comes into play on five holes, so if this is your first time playing here, your ball will get dunked. I guarantee it."

Par looked up at that comment to see how the new girl would react to water hazards.

Kim flinched, and her hand tightened around the grip of her putter.

Good, she's afraid of them.

"Remember, if the first two holes don't kill your score and confidence, the water on the back side can drown it. Last year I started with two sevens and was so demoralized, I muffed and topped balls all over the rest of the course. I ended up with a ninety-five, the worst round I've had since I was a kid."

Excellent. Get her psyched out, Brooke. Scare her by saying the sloped greens of eight and seventeen cause many three- and four-putts, and hitting off the tee on fifteen is like threading a needle to set yourself up for a clear shot over the water. Don't tell her that seven, ten, and thirteen are birdie opportunities.

"Seventeen is your longest par four, and be careful not to hit into the lagoon on your drive. Lay up and be happy with a bogey. If you hit it long, you might clear the water."

She's telling her too much, Par thought, as she dried off her Top-Flite golf balls.

"You end the round with a short dogleg that's surrounded by thick woods. Be happy finishing your round with a par on eighteen."

"Thanks. Now I'm really sorry I didn't play a practice round."

MEDALIST HONORS

A few minutes after seven thirty, Par walked to the first tee. She heard Liz Carlton's voice behind her: "Hey, Par. Wait up."

Par stopped. Liz came to her and hugged her tight. "I read that article. Boy, the *Cit Pat* had some nerve pairing your golf picture with the drunk-driving charge."

Par flinched at her last three words and stepped back. "I wasn't drunk, Liz."

"Good to hear that, but you've been scandalized publicly. Why did that happen?"

"I don't know. Maybe somebody down there doesn't like me."

"Or doesn't like your family."

Par felt dazed by the remark. She knew that being from a rich family bred jealousy in some people. She had felt it in high school, then lost it as she'd blended with coeds at MSU who came from families far richer than hers, especially on the golf team. She had played with country clubbers and avoided discussing her home course, a great course but nonetheless public. Henry Parker had refused to join the Country Club of Jackson because he didn't like to flaunt that he had money. Ironically, it was the country club that held the annual charity auction created in his memory to raise funds for the hospital and the community college. Par had always been the emcee at the event. Her mother said she envied Par's talent for public speaking. Par knew this compliment was a lie. Jitters made Par's voice tremble and her fingers quiver as she turned the pages of her notes. She knew her mother said that so she herself wouldn't have to do the job.

Heather Lane, already on the first tee, called out to them, "Hey, guys. It's time!"

"Forget it for now," Liz said.

Par shook like a dog after a bath, nodded her head. They pulled their carts up to where Heather had placed her alma mater's orange-and-blue golf bag near the left tee marker. Pulling a cart or carrying a bag automatically differentiated youth from the oldsters.

Liz and Par warmed up with a few stretches. When Heather exhaled a big sigh of impatience, Par said, "Let's get started."

They gathered in a circle, and Par twirled a blue tee in the air to drop into the center, designating their order of teeing off. It fell to the grass and pointed at Liz, so she would tee off first. Another toss, and it pointed at Par, so Heather would be last to drive on the first hole. Thereafter honors, the low score, would dictate the order in which they teed off.

The nerve-racking first shot of an eighteen-hole round. Par's heart beat fast; her stomach tied up in knots of self-doubt. She waited her turn at the slightly mounded tee box, staring at a divot. She breathed deeply to gain control and create calm energy, closed her eyes while Liz took a few practice swings. Then she heard the *smack.*

"Yikes! Be good, ball," Liz said.

Par opened her eyes and saw Liz scowling at the right rough. Not a good place to start. Liz walked off the tee box, and Par took her place. She plugged her tee into the grass with pressure from her palm and golf ball. She placed her driver gently on the grass behind the ball, stepped back, swung the club a few times to establish rhythm, returned to her address, and willed her backswing to be slow and follow through high. She smacked the ball 250 yards down the middle of the fairway.

"Great drive," Liz said.

"Thanks," Par said. The tension in her body dissolved. She left her tee bent into the grass, as was her custom and superstition on the first hole if her drive was long and straight. She considered it an offering to the golf goddess.

Heather set up between the tee markers. Taking no practice swings, she swung her driver back fast and hooked her ball into a bunker in the left rough.

"Damn," Heather said.

Par happily walked alone down the middle of the fairway, into the matutinal haze. She loved an early-morning tee time, loved hitting an approach shot onto a dew-topped green and watching it curve out an imprint, like a brushstroke. She'd putt through the wetness, hitting the ball with a firmness she would let up on after the sun had dried the greens. With her first putt, the golf ball rolled to the hole, trailed by a geyser of water. The brushstroke told no lies—it either ended in the hole or showed a pulled, pushed, short, or long stroke. On in regulation (two strokes below par), her first putt long, Par made the second putt for par and felt as if she had tamed one of the first two beasts.

The day heated up, the greens dried out, and Par ignored Naomi Chang's request to monitor Heather. With her confidence bolstered after posting par after par on the first eight holes, she stood on the ninth green, proud of the score that would be posted on the official scoreboard in the clubhouse for the rest of the field to see and fear. Then, as she stood over her two-foot putt, a distance she could normally drain with her eyes closed, an image of Pinky and Gail "together" came to her. She missed the putt and had a three-footer coming back. Luckily, she sank the comeback putt to save bogey. She cussed at herself for letting the outside in.

Liz shot a forty-one on the front side, and Heather said she shot a thirty-nine. The first threesome of the day—Hilary, Brooke, and Georgia—shot in the low forties, which made Par feel very satisfied with her one-over-par thirty-seven. The front nine was way tougher than the back, so Par counted on coming in under par on the second nine.

They all bought snacks in the clubhouse: PowerBars, hot dogs, Corn Nuts, and bottled waters. They ate as they walked to the tenth tee. There was never time to sit and have lunch between nines. Golfers had to maintain an even, steady pace.

After all three hit long, perfect drives and walked down the middle of the fairway together, Liz asked Par, "How's your mom?"

Par tightened her grip on the handle of her cart. "She's okay."

"Still a rabid Republican?"

Par laughed. "Some things never change." Par knew Liz's liberal politics and didn't want to have to defend her mother. "She's in California, visiting Joy."

"You're kidding. She's missing your golf week?"

"Yeah. I'll give you details after golf. It's complicated."

Liz nodded.

"What'd she do, find a surfer boyfriend out there?" Heather asked.

Par didn't look at Heather and answered, "A boyfriend. Right. She's sixty-eight years old. Give me a break." Par needed not to let the outside in. Why would Heather ask that? She clearly hadn't read about Par's arrest, or she'd be using it against Par right about now. Some players tried to find subjects that upset their opponents. She knew Liz wasn't the type, but Heather was capable of dirty play.

For her second shot, Par gripped her three-wood tight and swung fast, with disastrous results. She topped the ball, something good players did not do, and slammed her club head into the ground, something good players sometimes did.

"Touched a nerve, didn't I?" Heather said.

Par gave herself a quick mental lecture to keep cool and not lose concentration. A golfer did not want to show vulnerability. Remembering Nick's tip, she loosened her grip, slowed down her swing, and recovered with a perfect four-iron shot that landed in the center of the green and set her up for birdie. She looked at Heather and held back saying her thought: *Take that, Miss University of Florida.*

At fifteen, Par sunk a six-footer to save par and said, "Four."

"Six," said Liz.

"Four," said Heather.

As they walked off the green, Liz got Par's attention with a motion of her hand. The two walked a good distance behind Heather toward the next tee box. "She did not get a four. She had a bogey!" Liz hissed.

"Are you sure?" Par asked.

"Positive. She hit a good drive, pulled her second shot left of the green, was on in three, and two-putted for a five."

"Are you going to say something?"

"You're keeping her score," said Liz.

They stopped walking and looked at Heather at the next tee, wiping her hands with a towel.

"I can't. I don't want to add stress to this round. You know she'll deny it."

"We've got three holes left. If she pulls this again, I'm calling her on it."

Heather turned around and said, "Come on, you guys, the next threesome is on our tail. Par, I think you still have honors."

"I do. Give me a second." Par started to write down a four for Heather and stopped. "Heather, what'd you have again?"

"Four. Same as you."

Par wrote it down and wouldn't look at Liz.

On the back nine, Par's putter had been the best part of her game. She sank every putt within ten feet with the exception of seventeen, that devil of a hole. She three-putted on its sloped green for a double-bogey six and ended up with another one-over-par thirty-seven. She knew she could have done better on the back side. A couple of fat approach shots and bogeys on the two par-three holes had messed up her chances for a below-par round. She cautioned herself about complaining. Any round in the seventies on qualifying day was cause for happiness.

After the threesome attested scores, Par immediately walked into the clubhouse to see how the first threesome had done and the front-nine postings for the rest of the field. She saw a scowling Brooke Benson stomping around the clubhouse in her flashy outfit, slapping golf clothes on hangers while talking to someone on her cell phone. Looking at the scoreboard, Par saw that Brooke had posted an eighty-four. Par understood her foul mood and decided to stay out of her way.

Hilary Harris, the defending champ, posted an unexciting eighty.

Georgia had shot an eighty-six. There was danger in that score. She'd be paired with a low shooter from today on Tuesday.

"Pitiful, isn't it?" Georgia had come out of the restroom and stood next to Par.

"What happened?"

"My left wrist. Shooting pains the whole eighteen holes." She lifted her left hand up for Par to see a dirty golf towel holding ice wrapped around the pain.

"You forgot to take your pills, right?"

"Of course. Damn, I'm getting old."

"No, just forgetful." Par patted her on the back. "Remember them tomorrow. You'll need a healthy wrist 'cause you're probably playing Hilary."

Sam Walton, the course's marshal, was posting Par's score. He stopped for a moment to wink at Par, and she returned the gesture.

Sam had been one of the best senior players in Jackson before a stroke, three years earlier, had left him with some permanent paralysis on his left side. At seventy-five, he was still handsome and tan, energetic and good-natured, and still slicking back thick, wavy, dyed-black hair. He was a big fan of the women golfers, and the feeling was mutual.

"Hey, nice round," Georgia said, when he had written the 74 after Par's name. "You'll be tough to beat this week."

"As always," Sam said.

"We'll see if I can keep it going. You know how it can be."

Over the years, they had both seen other players shoot low rounds on Monday, then lose on Tuesday and suffer the dreaded consolation flight, where losers played other losers and whoever made it to Friday and won became the championship flight consolation winner, which really meant "winning loser of other losers." Par did not want that title.

With large tumblers packed with ice and a pitcher of Coke, Par's playing partners and Georgia sat with Hilary Harris at a long picnic table with a view of the eighteenth hole to watch the other championship-flight players approach their final green. This was a tradition.

"Where's Brooke?" Heather asked Hilary.

"Probably having a temper tantrum in her car. She'll be back."

They giggled.

Everyone had a reputation for something. Some golfers went quiet after a bad round. Some turned to beer. Some went home and took it out on their husband and kids. Some drove too fast. And some ate.

Par was the low shooter in the clubhouse, but she couldn't relax until the other ten players in the championship flight had all posted scores. She sipped her Coke, crossed a leg over a knee, leaned her back into the table's edge, and got ready to size up who was high and who was low as they walked toward the eighteenth green. She was most worried about Kelly Hayes and Kim Allen because they had posted front-nine scores of thirty-eight and thirty-seven, respectively.

There were signs of how well the round had gone for a golfer. If there was energy in her walk and a smile on her face. If she waved to the small gallery at the picnic table or avoided eye contact. If she quickly pulled a club out of her bag and hit a crisp second shot tight to the pin or if she had hooked her ball into the woods or hit long into the rough, then had to hit a low pitch shot under low-hanging limbs toward the green. If her chip shot came close to the hole or ran long. If she one-putted for birdie or three-putted for bogey (or worse). If she kicked her bag, pounded her club head into the grass, slammed a club into the bottom of her bag, uttered a cuss word, or placed hands on hips and stared hard at the green. All were signs.

Par watched Kelly Hayes walk toward a well-placed drive in the middle of the eighteenth fairway. Kelly took a long time figuring out what club to hit next (indecisiveness meant nervousness). Par enjoyed the show. When Kelly finally hit her approach shot, she hit it fat, digging up a huge divot in the process. She shoved the short iron into her bag and pulled her cap's brim down low while shaking her head in the fashion of *no, this can't be happening to me.*

Par felt relieved and crossed Kelly off her list of medalist contenders.

Liz nudged Par and said, "Maybe you'll be medalist."

"That's a big maybe. Wait until we see what the other youngsters and the new girl have done with the back nine."

"Want to place bets?" Heather asked.

Par ignored her and poured Coke refills for herself and Liz.

Casey Carter, the veteran sports writer, joined their group. He was tan and gaunt and had electric-blue eyes. He was handsome until he smiled—crooked teeth marred the perfection of his face. Casey sat next to Par and did something he never did with the women golfers. He put an arm around her and pumped it twice. She folded in toward his chest, never knew he was that strong.

"How'd it go today, ladies?" he asked as he let go of Par.

Par scooted a little sideways and sat up straight. "Pretty good. How are you doing?"

"Itchin' to write. Are you going to get the most ink, Par?"

"We'll see. I shot a seventy-four." She licked her lips wide and tasted salt from sweat and sweetness from the Coke.

"Nice round. How 'bout the rest of you?" He turned his body to look briefly at each player.

"Seventy-nine," Liz said.

"Seventy-seven," Heather said.

"Eighty," Hilary said. "I wasn't concentrating very hard. But my free ride's over. I'll get serious tomorrow."

"Eighty-six. My wrist was killing me."

"What happened?"

"Arthritis. I forgot to take my medicine," Georgia said.

"Tough luck," Casey said, as he jotted down the scores on his notepad. "Brooke, how 'bout you?"

"Eighty-four. My putter was broken."

"That's still a decent score," Casey said, then asked Par, "Who's your biggest threat?"

"Probably everyone still out there under thirty."

They all laughed.

Par twisted one of her bottom buttons. She knew that whatever she said could be quoted in the next day's paper. "And that new girl, Kim Allen." Par pointed to the fairway, to the woman in red and black standing near her ball, waiting for Rhonda Stein to chip onto the green. "Who knows what she's capable of?"

"I plugged her name into Google before coming here," Casey said, and flipped his notes to a previous page. "She won the New Mexico women's state amateur tournament when she was seventeen, and played four years with Arizona State. Her hometown newspaper boasted she was the next Nancy Lopez, but she had to stop playing for a few years because of carpal tunnel syndrome. She had surgery to correct it a few years ago."

"Why'd she move here?"

"Dunno. I'll be sure to ask her. Our new sports editor loves to print newcomer stories."

"Speaking of stories"—Par's voice turned to a whisper—"who's my enemy at the paper?"

"Don't know, but Jule is busy grilling every employee to find the snake and squeeze out its venom," Casey whispered back.

"Love it," Par said, as she leaned her shoulder into his.

"Shh. Let's watch this," he said.

Kim had a forty-yard wedge shot to the green. She pitched it to within four feet.

"Nice," Casey said.

A button came off in Par's hand. She tossed it under the table and sat on her hands, watching the action on the green.

Kim missed the putt, then coolly tapped in the six-inch putt for par. Walking away from the hole, she snatched off her visor and slapped its band against her thigh.

Casey smiled at Par and moved to the scorers' board to watch the threesome post their results.

The picnic table soon became crowded as more players finished their rounds. Par smelled sweat mixed with hints of stale perfume. Napkins were used to rub grass ends and dirt off sweaty ankles. In low voices, the women swapped stories about missed short putts and impossible under-the-lip sand-trap shots. They saved talk of their long birdie putts and holed-out chip shots in the hope that Casey would interview them and print the glorified details.

"Check it out. Christy's deep in the woods," Heather said.

The picnic-table gallery went silent, and everyone watched Christy Evans frantically look for her ball amid trees and brush. With her nonstop legs in a fuchsia skort, she was easy to follow. A lost ball would add a penalty stroke, and she'd have to return to the tee and hit another drive—one of the more painful ways to end a round.

"Found it!" Christy yelled to her playing partners.

"She'll never get out of there on her first try," Brooke said.

As Christy set up for her impossible shot, Par stood up to watch. Her fingers started in on another button. She had been in those woods two years ago, and it had taken her one whiff and two shots to get out. She'd ended up three-putting for an eight and losing the match.

Christy took little time setting up for the shot.

A *whack* sound made Par hold her breath. She expected to hear the knock of ball hitting tree. But no other sounds came, and everyone watched Christy's ball weave a low path through a thousand trees, roll through the sand trap, climb up and over the trap's high bunker, and land on the green, stopping six feet from the hole.

"My God, she's set up for birdie," Par said to Casey, who had returned to watch the action.

"Wow, helluva shot," Casey said, as he clicked his pen and began writing in his notepad.

"She must be living right to get such a lucky break," Heather said.

Par could tell, by the firm set of Christy's face and lack of glee expressed with fist-pumping action or looking into the sky, thanking the Big Guy for her luck, that her back-nine score would not place her in contention for medalist honors.

After all the scores were posted, Naomi Chang announced that

Par Parker-Swink had won medalist honors with her seventy-four. Second place went to Kim Allen and Danielle Parkinson, who had both shot seventy-fives. Par tingled with pride and relief as she accepted applause and pats on the back. She looked at Casey Carter, who motioned for her to come over to where he stood with the *Cit Pat's* photographer, a chubby, full-lipped guy wearing Oakley sunglasses, stud earrings, and rumpled clothes who didn't look old enough to handle the complexity of the big camera strapped around his neck.

"Congrats," they both said.

"Thanks, guys. I couldn't be happier."

"Let's go for some pictures of you on the green. Get a club—maybe we'll get an action shot," the boy said in a man's deep, bossy voice.

Par's energy surged. She had to will herself not to run toward her golf bag. *Control,* she thought. *Everyone's watching.* She grabbed the blade of her Bulls Eye putter and pulled it out of her bag. Walking to the eighteenth green toward the newspapermen felt like the good old days.

THE ENEMY

Par quickly took care of the Normans. She relaxed in her mother's favorite chair in the sitting room while reviewing what she had said to Casey about her birdies and putts to save par. A Norman rubbed against her shins and jumped onto her lap. She rested her feet on the ottoman, stroked the cat absentmindedly, and surveyed her mother's bowling trophies stacked on two shelves. Adele had become a two-league-a-week bowler after Joy left town. She'd come home around midnight after bowling, cheeks flushed and clothes smelling like cigarette smoke. She'd go straight to the laundry room, pull off her tan slacks and black-and-tan polyester shirt (her name inscribed near her heart), and run a small load in the washing machine. Then she'd shower and watch the rest of *Johnny Carson* in the den.

One time when Par came home late from a date, she sat and watched TV with Adele. During a commercial, she asked her mom what she loved about bowling. Adele turned her whole body toward Par and said, "I love being in a bowling alley." She went on to describe how bowling stimulated all her senses: fingers sliding into the holes of her ball and the hefty weight of it in her palm, watching the graceful slide and follow-through of bowlers on adjacent lanes, hearing balls smack lane boards and the rumbling clatter of pins after a strike, seeing the language of bodies bending and twisting to influence a spare and the grimaces when the ball went cleanly between a split, smelling spilled beer and fried food, and eating overcooked, thin burgers and deep-fried, breaded mushrooms.

In an uncharacteristic moment of blissful connection, she asked Par, "What do you love about golf?" Excited about her mother's attention, Par thought for a moment. "I love the finesse of it, the strategy of playing each hole smart, the shot making, adapting to weather, analyzing my competitors' strengths and weaknesses. I love the fact that I can outdrive a man twice my size. There are always surprises in every round, surprises like sinking a long birdie putt, skipping the ball over water, getting a favorable bounce away from a hazard, holing out a chip shot, and the ultimate—making a hole in one."

"A hole in one. What are the odds?"

"Probably a million to one."

"And you've had two."

Par nodded. She had her mother's full attention and didn't want to stop. "I love the thrill of winning. I love the press and the attention from people, even strangers, for what I do myself and not for being the daughter of Mr. Chevrolet."

Par held her breath because Johnny had come back on and she

didn't want to look at the TV. She wanted to tell her mother about first-hole jitters, how she hated her golfer's tan, and how she sometimes felt like an oddball for playing golf all summer—away from her peers—with older women with jobs, husbands, and kids, but Adele swiveled her body back to watch the show.

* * *

At home, Par placed the Top-Flite #1 golf ball she had played the day's round with into an empty cubbyhole in the wooden display cabinet her father had crafted. It had seven horizontal rows with seven compartments in each row and hung on a wall in her trophy room. She saved golf balls from memorable, low rounds throughout her golf career. Only three empty spaces remained. Henry used to marvel at the fact that there wasn't a scratch on any of the golf balls, even though she had played eighteen holes with each one, hit it seventy-some times. When you continuously hit the club's sweet spot, there wouldn't be a cut or mark on the ball.

All the balls were white. Par had never accepted the wacky trend of colored golf balls. She was too much of a traditionalist, and it hurt her sensibilities to see neon yellow, pink, green, or orange balls soar off a tee and bounce down the fairway.

She gave a thumbs-up gesture to Isadora and imitated her arms-raised-in-joy movement.

Par swam a few laps and sipped a glass of lemonade poolside, and after she had basked in memories of the day—medalist honors, an interview with Casey Carter, accolades from the other golfers, her cheeseburger basket "on the house" at the Water Hazard—she felt an emptiness and a sense of failure that rattled her sense of victory.

Would the article by Casey Carter and her picture on the sports page be big enough to assuage her humiliation? Would it change the public's negative perception of her? Would the public even read it? Well, the sports fans would. She knew Casey had given her that hug because he felt sorry for her and wanted to show he was on her side. But a bigger issue loomed. When would she feel better about herself? These questions attacked her mind, and she did not like it.

The portable phone in the cabana rang. Par ran inside. It was Pinky.

"I did it. I'm the medalist!" Par blurted, trying to return to her good mood.

"Hold on for a second . . . I'm putting you on speakerphone . . . Gail's here, too . . . Okay, remind me again, what does that mean?"

"I shot the lowest score of the day, which is an honor, and it pairs me tomorrow with a high shooter in the championship flight." Par returned to the patio.

"So, you'll win easily tomorrow, right?" they said in unison.

Irritated with the speakerphone and upset that her two friends were speaking simultaneously, Par kicked at the water in the pool. "Well, I wouldn't say it will be easy. Christy Evans had a bad day today, and she could come back hot tomorrow."

"One day at a time, my dear," Pinky said.

"Yes, that's what they say." Par began walking around the pool.

"We've been thinking a lot about you. We know you don't like change, and—"

"That's nice," Par interrupted. "I've been trying not to think about you two. I don't want to talk about your situation right now, okay? I have victory on my mind, and I need peaceful thoughts to get me through this week."

She heard Pinky muffle the mouthpiece and exchange indistinct words with Gail. Par squeezed the phone, trying to hear better.

Pinky shouted, "Two things. Beat Christy tomorrow, and go read the letters to the editor right now. You've got some outraged fans in this city." *Click.*

Par hustled to the front door for the newspaper. As her fingers quivered, she found the section. Jule Gladstone had prefaced the letters with an acknowledgment the newspaper had made an error. She expressed regret that an employee stepped out-of-bounds to publicize Ms. Parker's "alleged" offense.

Dear Editor,

How could you stoop so low as to splash Par Parker's unfortunate arrest on the front page of our paper? Why would you put her sweet golf picture with the shaming article and tout TOP LADY GOLFER BUSTED FOR *DUI? That was cheap. Par Parker is from one of the best families in this town. Her father, rest his soul, was a man of integrity and generosity to this community. His foundation, started after his death, assists and inspires people who are less fortunate. This is no way to treat his daughter. You should be ashamed!*

Maxine and Albert Henderson

Dear Editor,

I've bought a Chevrolet every two years from Parker Chevrolet since 1966. Henry Parker was a close friend of mine. Printing the news of Par Parker's arrest, without a conviction, is simply slanderous. The Citizen Patriot is not the National Enquirer. Or is it?

Mike Moses

Dear Editor,

It was an unconscionable act for the Citizen Patriot to print the details of Par Parker's alleged DUI with an archived golf photo on the front page of our newspaper. You've violated journalistic protocol and defamed an outstanding person of our community. Unless you print an apology to Par Parker for everyone to read, I'm canceling my subscription.

Professor Emeritus Edward Murphy

Dear Editor,

Thank you for reporting the drinking problem of Par Parker, daughter of Adele and the late Henry Parker. Your article shows that the abuse of alcohol spares no family. Regardless of socioeconomic background, alcoholism can kill. Ms. Parker is lucky she did not hurt anyone, or she'd be looking at doing time in our prison north of town and some poor family would be suffering a loss they'd never get over.

Mrs. Anthony McCormac
President of MADD (local chapter)

Dear Editor,

I've known Par Parker since grade school. She does not drink to excess. You were wrong to put her picture in the paper under that sensationalistic headline!

Amanda (Pinky) King

Standing very still in the foyer, Par said, "Wow." Turning her face toward the mirror, she saw a puzzled look. She wasn't sure how to feel. Relieved? Vindicated? Or more on display and embarrassed?

Par called Jule Gladstone.

"Jule, it's Par. I just read the letters to the editor."

"Good. Do they help?"

"A little. And thanks for your note."

"You are so welcome, dear, and I'm glad you called. I found out who placed the story about you."

Par sat down on a lawn chair. "Do I want to know?"

"You tell me."

"Okay, tell me." She held her breath.

"My cousin Otto is a copy editor, and I hate to say it, but he took a bribe from a newsroom clerk to write the article and place an archived golf picture with it. Travis, the clerk, wanted it on the front page, and Otto earned an extra tip for that."

"Does your cousin need the money that badly?"

"Black sheep of the family. Demoted as a reporter two years ago. He's an alcoholic, thrice divorced, with six kids. They've both been fired."

"Who's Travis and what's he got against me?"

"He's Travis Bane, Par."

"Bane." Par's brain sifted through its Rolodex. "Oh my God, that's Louie's son, isn't it?"

"Yes."

"Damn." Par remembered Mrs. Bane at the trial: dark, frizzy hair, big eyes, a jutting chin. Every day, Doris Bane had worn no makeup, no stockings, and the same dingy gray shift dress. With her brood of four boys, she had arrived early and stayed late. The skinny Bane boys, with buzz cuts, ranged in age from four to sixteen. They looked as if they were trying too hard to be grown-up, in white shirts and black neckties loosely knotted underneath confused and tired faces. Par was sure the boys, who didn't miss a day of the trial, were a ploy to gain sympathy from the jury. During closing comments, Par nearly went mad listening to the pitiful defense of temporary insanity based on Louie's enormous debt and sickly wife.

No matter. The trial was swift. The headline BANE GETS LIFE! spread across the front page of the newspaper. Even for first-degree murder, Michigan law did not allow the death penalty. Par remembered thinking how unfair it was that those four boys continued to have a father who was alive.

"There's one more thing, Par."

"What?" Par tensed.

"Travis got the lowdown about your arrest from Deputy Virgil."

"Why would she do that?" Par yelled into the phone.

"They're dating."

"Dating?" She did the math in her head. "She must like the young ones."

"I would expect the sheriff to come down hard on her if you turn her in."

"If I turn her in? I'm calling Sheriff Conrad right now. Thank you so much."

In shock, Par raced into the house and punched in the private number for Sheriff Douglas Conrad. She had kept her father's little black book in a secret drawer at her desk. His voice mail message referred callers to his deputy sheriff until he returned from vacation. She hung up and decided not to communicate with his second-in-command.

Rereading the letters to the editor and knowing there'd be an article in the paper the next day about her low golf round made her feel better. Par wanted to celebrate with a friend who had not become a changeling, and she had a craving for Cajun whitefish.

She called Carmen and set up a six o'clock dinner with husbands at Daryl's, the most upscale restaurant downtown at the moment. It was hard to change a small town's pedestrian culinary tastes, but Daryl's and its eclectic cuisine had lasted six years so far, surprising everyone except Daryl himself.

* * *

Nick made a toast. "To the best golfer in town."

Glasses clinked. Par felt relaxed and happy.

Blake offered another toast. "Those letters to the editor were great. You've been redeemed."

All glasses clinked again.

"Do you think?" Par asked.

"Yeah, except for that one, but Mrs. McCormac has a burden of grief she'll never get over," Blake said.

"Her son, you know," Carmen said.

"Only child," Blake said, as he reached across the table to touch Carmen's hand.

"Yes. I can't imagine the loss," Par said. She thought about Isadora.

The waitress poured everyone water and must have felt the sadness at the table, because she didn't say a word.

"I saw that Pinky got a little press today," Carmen said to Par, with a nudge.

"Yeah, and I found out who got that article about me printed."

"Who?" Blake asked.

"Travis Bane."

Blank faces all around.

"The son of the bastard who killed my father."

"Oh dear," Carmen said.

"Why didn't you tell me?" Nick asked.

"Payback time," Blake said.

"What do you mean, *payback time?* I never did anything to Travis Bane."

"But he may think you were partly responsible for putting his father in the big house. He was just a kid at the time, right?" Blake said.

Nick thumped his fist on the table. "How did he do it?"

"The little brat works, or did work, at the *Cit Pat.* Jule Gladstone fired him and his accomplice." She sipped her drink to calm down.

"Who helped him?" Nick asked.

"A cousin of Jule's. A copy editor. Can you believe that?"

"Why'd he do it?"

"He's a loser, so deep in debt he took a bribe from Bane."

"That's kind of pitiful," Carmen said.

"Blake, I never did a thing to that kid," Par said, pointing a finger at him.

Blake held up his hands as if they were a catcher's mitt.

"It's mean of him to lash out at you for something his father did," Carmen added.

Par swiveled to face Carmen. "He must have gotten a twisted account of the Parkers from his mother."

"I'm sorry, Par. I said the wrong thing."

"Oh, forget it, Blake. We're here for a good time. Let's eat and get me home to bed early for my match tomorrow."

The crowd of diners and poor acoustics forced Carmen and Par to lean close together to talk, while Nick focused on drinking his pitcher of beer and Blake drank what Par called his "girly" drink, a Grasshopper. They ate crab nachos, everybody's favorite appetizer.

Carmen said, "Gail called me today."

Par's body tensed. "What'd she say?"

Carmen said nothing for an eternity.

"Come on, I can handle it," Par said, as she pushed her small plate off to the side.

"She's telling Jesse tonight."

"No!" Par banged her fist on the table. Nick and Blake looked at her with startled expressions. She waved them off and said, "Never you mind."

"Don't overreact. We have to support her," Carmen said.

"The hell we do. I'm calling her right now. Can I use your cell? I left mine at home."

"What are you going to say?"

"To be honest, I need her to wait until after I win this tournament." Par saw she had the guys' attention. She whispered in Carmen's ear, "Jesse could hurt her. I don't want to worry about Gail's well-being right now."

"Come on, this isn't junior high," Nick said, with a hint of sarcasm.

"So, you're making this about you," Carmen said to Par.

"Yes, I am." Par snatched Carmen's purse and hustled to the bathroom. She hated hearing people talk on cells in a public restroom's stall, but she dialed the number and was prepared to irritate anyone peeing next to her.

Gail picked up on the third ring, which felt like the third day. Before she said hello, Par said, "Gail."

"Yes?"

"Please, please, please don't tell Jesse tonight."

No comment.

"Oh, Christ. You've already told him."

No comment.

"Is he right there?"

"Yes. And no, I haven't. I've changed my mind. Please take me off your list. I am not interested in buying your insurance." She hung up.

The drama. The acting. Gail talked so fast. Par hoped she heard right—that she had not told Jesse and was not going to tell him.

* * *

Carmen was the only one who ordered dessert, a slice of cheesecake. Par and Blake drank coffee. Nick had switched to scotch and water.

On the way home, and close to the community college, Par glanced at her side mirror and saw a car tailing the Tahoe. "Nick, there's a cop behind you. Slow down."

He tapped the brake. "I'm going the speed limit."

The tailgater swerved left and gunned the pedal to swerve around their car.

"It's Dee Dee," Nick said, and gave her a nod of recognition.

Par stared ahead. "I am so glad you are driving. She's a nut case."

Relieved to be home, and a little light-headed, but energized, Par decided to dry off seat cushions around the pool after the second thunderstorm in two days. Fetching towels from the cabana, she walked in on Joey and P. C. cuddled under a lightweight blanket on the sofa. She mumbled something about the rain and quickly walked out.

Wiping down the plastic cushions, she thought Joey should have taken P. C. home by now. "Out of my control," she said to crickets and the thick night air. "I need to be a good mom and let them be."

Tired but not sleepy, she went into Todd's room. Elmo and

Cookie Monster hand puppets sat on two headposts. She smiled, slipped her hand into Cookie Monster's head, moved his mouth; in her head, she heard Todd's voice saying, *Me want cookie!*

But that was so long ago. She replaced the puppet on the post, then looked at the collage Todd had created with pictures he had taken of Squeeze. Her two favorite pictures were of Squeeze with a shuttlecock in his mouth, thinking he had some skill to show off during a party where the guests had played badminton; and standing on the diving board before one of his graceless dives into the pool. *Oh, I miss that dog.*

Par blew dust off the top of four high school yearbooks stacked horizontally. They vied for space on Todd's dresser next to a collection of Asimov's *The Robot* series. She had been disappointed that he read science fiction—took that to mean he needed to escape to worlds that did not exist, and what did that mean? Sitting on his bed, she absent-mindedly drummed her fingers on his mattress. For the first time in a year, she was happy he wasn't home. At the last minute, he had decided to attend summer quarter at Central Michigan University (she suspected a girlfriend) instead of working with his father to make money for his new passion, snowboarding.

Should she tell him of her arrest? If so, how? By phone, postcard, e-mail, or letting the gossip naturally spread north? She hated Todd's one-e-mail-per-week rule. When he had first left home, she had gone a little crazy with instant messaging. Todd had become irritated; he'd told her to "get a grip" and stop popping in at him on the computer so many times a day. After that, she had tried to carefully craft her weekly e-mail, considering whether to offer advice, or encouragement, or money; to ask questions about his classes or friends; or to write about the weather or the small goings-on around the Parker-Swink household.

No. He didn't need to know the bad news. She resolved to call him after winning the tournament.

Par logged on to the Internet to send Joy a note about her medalist honors. Adele might not be in town to enjoy her golf news, but she could still be in the loop. Par needed her to know that she had shot the lowest round.

Her inbox showed an e-mail from Joy with the subject *Mom Cut Her Hair!* Par braced her insides and clicked on the message, then quickly clicked on the attachment: Adele with her gray hair cut. Cut short-short. It was wavy, and it stuck out from her crown. It made her look twenty years younger. Par's eyes froze on the picture. The look on her mother's face was *Look at what I've done—I couldn't feel better.* There was also a look of challenge in her expression. Her lipstick was orchid pink, and copper-wire earrings with multicolored glossy beads dangled from her earlobes. Adele had never before worn dangly earrings.

Par's breath went rapid. She twisted a button. Adele must have gone mad on that California sunshine. She reread Joy's e-mail, clicked on the picture again, reread the e-mail, and went back and forth many times.

Hey, Sis. Look at the new Adele! She's eating salads with champagne vinaigrette dressing, sampling sushi and loving it, riding the Ferris wheel, and drinking Lemon Drops. This Norman guy is real sweet. I think you'll like him. She's the first in a long line of Minkowski women to cut their hair short (pic attached).

She's using vinaigrette dressing. Ranch dressing had been a staple in Adele's meals. It always broke Par's heart when she fixed a meal for her mother, and—it didn't matter if it was macaroni and cheese or prime rib—Adele smothered everything on her plate with the white slop.

Her mother had changed.

Par went into a whirl, as if she had swum into a riptide. She wanted to grab on to the shoulders of those she loved to say, *Stop, hold still!*

Her fingers moved fast on the keyboard:

I won medalist honors today shooting a seventy-four. Tell your mother.

She clicked Send.

THE CHEATER, THE WINNERS, THE BABIES

After the first blank minute of morning wakefulness, Par's mind filled with gloom as she remembered Joy's e-mail. What was going on with her mother? Par had barely slept thinking Adele might not come home, or might bring this Norman home, and about more changes she had no control over interfering with her life. Maybe she should just stay in bed forever, forfeit the match to Christy. They couldn't make her play.

She didn't hear a sound in the house, which meant Nick and Joey had gone to work. She ducked under the sheet. No part of her wanted to walk eighteen holes in the humid heat, playing badly because she was tired. But losing today would put her in the consolation flight on Wednesday, and that would feel as bad as jail.

After a few minutes of feeling sorry for herself, Par knew she could never forfeit a match, and deep down, she knew she'd beat Christy. She forced herself to get up.

Arriving at the course fifteen minutes before her tee time, she had to skip her putting-practice routine. *Just as well,* she thought. Why tempt the golfers already there to talk to her about the letters to the editor? Surely those players who had missed her DUI write-up had read the letters.

She bought a cup of coffee, cooling it with fountain water to drink it fast. On her way to the first tee, without a glance at the golfers milling about the clubhouse and putting green, she ate a cinnamon donut. Pulses of anger shot through her body. "Fine, Mom. You live your life any way you want. Just forget about me," she said sotto voce. She hoped to fuse the angry energy with her desire to beat Christy, and to stay the hell out of that losers' flight.

Christy Evans was already at the tee box, sitting on a bench, tightening her cleats. She was very feminine and did not tone down her Cheryl Tiegs look for the golf course. She wore more makeup than all the other golfers put together. Her dangly earrings got a workout with every swing. She wore skorts and tight polo shirts tucked in. Par liked Christy. Liked being around her carefree spirit.

On the front nine, Par took long strides down each fairway, following her long drives, and sank long putts that amazed her tired self. Christy had had another bad golf day, hitting her ball consistently into the rough and sand traps and suffering through many missed short putts. Adding to Christy's misery and increasing Par's confidence in winning, Christy threw up while in the rough on two holes. Par thought she was suffering from a hangover, for Christy enjoyed her margaritas and was a night person, after all. Par even started rooting for her to make a putt—a very noncompetitive, non-Par thing to do.

With a comfortable lead—four up after nine holes—Par thought she could afford some sympathy toward this pretty young woman, newly married to a rookie cop who worked the graveyard shift, which had to be worrisome. Par suggested she buy some crackers to help settle her stomach, and that she drink warm water, not cold.

But Christy did not buy the crackers, did not drink water, and did not sink any crucial putts on the back nine.

Par ended the match at fourteen by sinking a fifteen-foot putt for par. She was five up with four holes left. They shook hands. Christy's grip was limp, and she requested they walk in, rather than play the remaining four holes.

With the pressure of competition off, Christy told Par she was pregnant. "I found out a week ago, and I'm not sure it's what I want at this point in my life." She looked at Par as if requesting advice.

"If you don't mind my asking, weren't you using birth control?"

"I blew it. Forgot some pills a few days. It was stupid and careless."

This is the beginning of her perfect body getting out of shape, Par thought. All the young girls could tuck in their shirts, while the older women covered extra weight around their middle by wearing shirts untucked.

"How does your husband feel about it?"

"Haven't told him," Christy replied in a tone that did not encourage more questions.

This conversation made Par's victory taste a little less sweet.

Later, in the clubhouse, she saw the pro Johnny Mitchell, Liz, and Heather standing in one corner. Heather had her arms crossed tightly over her chest. Liz's hands were fanned out on her hips. Par wondered if it had finally come to a showdown and walked over to the golf-shirt display closest to them, ostensibly to buy something, though she never wore that type of shirt.

Expressed rancor was rare for golfers who suffered the dignity of a sport steeped in politeness and reserved demeanor. That suffering typically manifested itself in behaviors like club waggling, OCD touching of clubs, ritualistic address of the ball, using the same penny or dime or pink plastic disc to mark the ball's place on the green, using only blue tees, wearing the same shirt for luck, or placing the golf bag at the same spot on each tee box on every hole.

Par eavesdropped.

"We were even at the end of eighteen. I'm ready for a playoff," Heather said.

"No, I won fourteen with a par. We tied the last four holes. That made me one up. That means I won the match," Liz said.

"You're scared of a playoff, that's all."

"Wait. I want to hear what happened, shot for shot, for Heather on fourteen. Liz?" Johnny asked.

Liz confirmed a drive in the rough; a second shot, hit thin, that dribbled into the fairway; a short-iron hit to the right of the green; a pitch shot onto the green; and one putt for bogey. Heather confirmed the same shots but excluded the dubbed shot and said she had hit a long-iron to the right of the green.

"Either of you have a caddie?" Johnny asked.

"I do. Christopher Wellington. He's drinking a pop over there." Liz pointed to where he sat, looking at pictures on the wall of Mike and Dave Hill. "He plays golf for Lumen Christi. He's also an honor student," Liz said.

"Yeah, I know him. I'll be just a minute." Johnny walked over to talk to Christopher.

Heather said, "You are really something. He's not going to take a kid's word against mine. Why are you being like this?"

"Save it. Let's wait and see." Liz stuffed her hands into her pockets.

Par placed a medium-size red shirt up against her chest to check the fit, then refolded it slowly. Liz and Heather stared out the window.

Johnny returned to give his verdict. "Heather, Christopher confirmed the five shots as Liz described. That hole goes to Liz. There'll be no playoff. Liz wins the match." With that he turned and gave the information to Naomi Chang, who had just walked into the clubhouse.

Heather walked out, muttering unprintable words.

Liz walked over to Par. "Did you enjoy the show?"

"You did absolutely great. You've busted her," Par said.

"I don't think it was worth it," Liz said, as she chewed a fingernail.

"Well, we'll see how she reacts. Maybe it will reform her."

"I wonder what Casey will write about it. I don't want her reputation ruined. There's nothing to be gained by that."

"I can relate." Par was also glad she'd had no part in calling Heather on her cheating.

* * *

Out of the sixteen players in the championship flight, eight winners remained in contention and eight losers dropped into the consolation flight. Kim Allen beat Brooke Benson, one of the twenty-somethings. Suzie Mangussi, the country club snob, lost to Rhonda Stein; Kelly Hayes and Danielle Parkinson, two young hotshots, battled each other three extra holes in a sudden-death playoff, before Kelly clinched a win with a birdie on the par-three third hole. The two upsets of the day involved oldsters beating youngsters. Georgia Davis clinched a win over Hilary Harris, the defending champion, one up on the eighteenth, and Lucy Gutowski had the best round of her life, defeating Ashley Crawford two up after seventeen. On Wednesday, Par would play Beth Finnegan, who trumped Joyce Fitzgerald three and two.

The first day's matches seemed to be a good omen for the older players. Par saw possible headlines in her mind that Casey could run in Wednesday's paper:

> Women's Match-Play Surprises
> Youngsters Get Walloped
> Sudden-Death Playoff!

Par didn't mind not being in the headline. Her win over Christy paled as a story. It was a mere stepping-stone toward the finals on Friday, where she expected—after winning—to get front sports-page billing. Par was happy for her win, knew she'd been lucky starting the round with four pars and an unlikely birdie on five. The tiredness she had felt after little sleep dissolved with "good shot" energy, and she managed to shove her troubles aside.

Walking to the parking lot, pulling her golf cart, Par noticed the quiet. Before rubber spikes had become mandatory, she had loved to hear the clacking sounds of her metal-spiked golf shoes on a paved cart path. She missed the noise and the distraction it provided from the quiet pressure that was golf. Next to her Tahoe, she saw Suzie Mangussi putting her clubs into the trunk of her Infiniti. Suzie was tall, narrow at the shoulders and wide at the hips. Unlike any other golfer's hands in this tournament, her hands were perfectly manicured, with short fingernails polished burnt orange to match her freckled skin. She had a six handicap and a reputation as a poor sport because she habitually rattled change in her pocket when an opponent was over a clinch putt. She had played on a public course only for this one tournament; otherwise, she dominated play at the Jackson Country Club, having won that course's women's championship for many of the past fifteen years, getting little competition from the ranks of the rich and pampered.

Suzie slammed her trunk closed and said, "I read about your drinking problem, Par. My ex-husband's brother has two DUIs. One more, and they'll send him to the big house."

Par hated her at that moment. "I don't have a drinking problem. I had some bad luck that night." Par heaved her bag and cart into the Tahoe's cargo hold. She slid into the driver's seat, rolled down the window to let out some of the steamy heat, and flicked on the AC.

"Right, that's what Lenny has been saying all along," Suzie yelled.

Par snapped her head toward Suzie, ready with a comeback, but the Infiniti's tires spun gravel dust, smothering her insult: "Good luck tomorrow in the losers' flight!"

* * *

The newspaper article about Monday's golf round was extra special to Par. Sports section, second page, top left. The twenty-eight-point headline: PAR PARKER SHOOTS 74 FOR MEDALIST HONORS. The two column–by–four inch picture: a big smile as she looked at her putter blade, with the caption DAZZLING PUTTING MAKES A MEDALIST. The article included many complimentary details about Par's qualifying round. Casey scattered three quotes from her in the text: "My short game is better than it's ever been. . ."; "I want to win this week to establish a record of ten wins. . . "; "Kim Allen played real well, and she could be a threat."

At the end of the article, he wrote about Hilary Harris's match the next day with Georgia Davis: twentysomething to fiftysomething. He also wrote a short bio about Kim Allen. Kim came from New Mexico, had played for Arizona State University, struggled with carpal tunnel pain, and had moved to Jackson with her partner, a senior design engineer with MACI, Jackson's largest manufacturer.

Par carefully cut out the picture and article, snipping just above the Kim Allen bio, and placed it on the butcher-block island so that Nick and Joey would notice it. Later she'd make copies for her mother and Todd.

She knew there'd be another article the next day, about her decisive win over Christy. To celebrate, she pulled steaks out of the freezer for Nick to grill and made a special trip to Culinary Secrets for wine, where she bought a bottle of California cabernet the staff had reviewed as "a sturdy, complex monster begging for steaks."

Before pulling out of the parking lot, Par saw a couple holding hands and walking on the side of the road. They looked odd together—his long, hairy legs made him over six feet tall; the top of the woman's head barely came up to his rib cage. He had messy brown hair and wore white dazzle basketball shorts with a silver vertical stripe at the side, and a loose-fitting Detroit Tigers tank top. His woman looked much older, with stiff gray hair and too-short shorts revealing cellulite and big knees. Her tight red scoop-neck top exposed the outline of a push-up bra and inches of flesh and cleavage. It looked like the woman was taking her breasts out for a walk.

They both wore sunglasses and flip-flops. When they walked

nearer her car, Par slipped on her shades to watch them discreetly. She noticed a snake tattoo band on the woman's right arm.

As they walked past, Par's brain made a shutter-quick identification of the woman. It was Dee Dee. In civilian clothes. Par recognized the walk.

And Travis Bane. She tightened her grip on the steering wheel, pressed harder on the brake, clenched her teeth. "Do not run them over. Do not," she told herself. When her fury calmed, she drove away in the opposite direction of her enemies.

* * *

Grabbing garden shears and a basket out of the garage, Par walked straight to the raised beds along the north side of her backyard patio. She snipped spinach leaves, gathered cucumbers, pulled a beefsteak tomato off its stem, and polished it clean on her shorts and ate it while taking her bounty into the kitchen. For dinner, she made her favorite spinach-grapefruit-avocado salad.

In a vengeful mood, Par called Larry Knight. She twisted a button after being put on hold.

"Knight," he said.

"Hello, I'm Par Parker, and you came highly recommended by—"

He interrupted her. "Yes, I've been expecting your call. Had a little chat with Jule Gladstone. You called the right guy."

"I don't know if you can help, but I feel fairly certain that I wasn't impaired last Friday night. I did coast through the stop sign, so I deserved a ticket."

"Give me the short version of what happened, and we'll make an appointment to discuss strategy."

"After some kind of penlight test, I blew into a short plastic tube. Dee Dee Virgil, the deputy—I knew her in high school, and there was no love between us—checked the result and announced I was just over the limit."

"Fantastic. She blew it by giving you a field Breathalyzer test. Pun intended." He chuckled. "It never holds up in court. She should have taken you to the hospital for a blood draw. That's the only way to prove your BAC was over the limit."

"BAC?"

"Blood alcohol content. Check your calendar, and let's get you in here."

She made an appointment for the first week of August. The lawyer's enthusiasm and optimism infused Par with the same. The damage from negative publicity couldn't be changed or stricken from the record. She'd live with that, but she wanted to keep her subbing job, and if people brought up the arrest, she could explain what had really happened.

* * *

At dinner, Joey ate a large T-bone, three helpings of salad, and half a loaf of garlic bread. He never looked up from his plate, and he ate fast. Par and Nick stared at him and ate little. Par's thoughts turned dark. She knew Joey ate when upset, whereas Todd fasted. When he finished his feast, Joey made a declarative statement that would forever change the way Par considered her youngest child: "P. C. is pregnant."

"No way," Nick said.

"Way," Joey replied, and looked at his mother. His expression mixed up his child face with a newly serious adult face that Par recalled having seen when he had returned from canoeing. She felt her stomach churn and her face flush in anger. Fighting tears, she pushed her chair back hard to stand up, and it tipped over. She wiped her mouth with a napkin and threw it at Joey and yelled, "You dumb kid! You've just ruined your life."

He swatted the napkin to the floor. "Worse than you've ruined yours? I love her," he yelled back.

"Love. You can't know anything about love. You're seventeen years old. . . and I suppose you'll want to marry the girl . . . a girl with lazy welfare parents . . . a girl who probably can't cook."

Par spat out these words in staccato fashion. This was the last thing she needed in her lousy life. She flashed back on images of Joey sniffing the fingers of his right hand at the dinner table in between bites and while watching late-night TV. He seemed to have a fascination with those two fingers. He was smelling her! Of course that would be a fixation for him.

Joey stood up and said, "Don't criticize her. You don't know anything about her life. She's cooked meals for her family since she was nine years old."

Who is this boy? Par wondered. She felt like yanking up his sagging cargo shorts to his armpits to hurt him and ruin his chances of having sex again. But she couldn't destroy youth like that. She had screwed up her son's chances at a normal life. She should have been complimentary about his girlfriend. Weren't teenagers attracted to what their parents didn't like or didn't approve of? She thought about Allen Gaines from high school.

Nick, the voice of reason all of a sudden, said, "Have you two decided what you'll do?"

Joey sat back down. "She's got that chess tournament in Ann

Arbor in two weeks that she's pretty nervous about. When she gets back, we'll figure it out. I think I want to work full-time with you."

Construction! The word blew Par's mind. She closed her eyes tight, fought for control. No career for a boy like Joey. She envisioned him with pulled muscles from lifting lumber, smashed fingernails from hammering, falling off a roof, or, God forbid, slicing off a body part with the blade of a circular saw. "What about college?" she pleaded.

"I don't need a degree to work with Dad."

Par regretted everything at that moment—being married, having children, being born into the Parker family.

"Where will you two live?" She felt a need to keep asking questions to stay connected.

"We'll get an apartment. We'll manage." He scanned the table. There was nothing left to eat. He drank the rest of his milk and asked, "May I be excused?"

He hadn't asked that question since puberty.

Par righted her chair and sat down. "You may leave the table, but you are not excused." She gripped the arms of her chair and felt a searing heat in her body.

Joey glared at her.

"You will go to hell for this," she snapped.

Joey jerked as if he had been slapped in the face. His eyes flicked toward Nick, who blurted, "I'll talk to Grandpa about bringing you into the business."

"Thanks, Dad." Joey walked toward the front door. Par stared at his back, at the back of the boy she had lost. He yelled, "You're wrong, Mom" and grabbed his car keys off a hook in the foyer while shoving the door open to leave.

Par and Nick looked at each other.

"How could you say that to him?" Nick shouted.

"How could he do this to us?" Par shouted back. She rushed out to the pool, kicked off her flip-flops, and sent them flying like a line drive to third base. They banged against the cabana's door. She dove in with her clothes on and thrashed through a few laps, splashing water out of the pool. When she stopped swimming to catch her breath, she saw Nick walk out onto the patio. He looked lost.

"Maybe it isn't his baby," she said as her chest heaved.

"Par, they've been going together for months now. I don't think he'd claim it if he had doubts. That's not something guys do." He put on a seersucker hat, his pool hat.

She pushed hair away from her face. "I thought you gave him the talk. Didn't you say to be responsible with birth control?"

"Shh. Not so loud . . . I told him. I also gave him a box of rubbers, magnum size and lubricated, though at that age they don't need the lube."

She spoke in a mean whisper: "This is worse than my getting locked up. People will think we're rotten parents." She wriggled out of her clothes and plopped them onto the tile of the patio. "Is he going to finish high school?" She slapped the water. "What about her? She's brainy, and now nothing will come of her. How can they take care of a baby?" She did not pause for an answer. "They're kids themselves." She hollered and swam another lap. Pausing at the shallow end, she said, "P. C. should give the baby up. No abortion. God, I hate abortion." She shuddered. "She can have it, then give it up."

Nick grabbed the skimmer and bounced the edge of the net's frame on the coping. He shook his head.

Par continued. "Those two shouldn't ruin three lives. Or four, if it's twins. Twins run in her family, you know."

He tossed the skimmer aside, picked up a blue rubber ring, and slammed it into the water at the deep end. "You know, they could live in our basement for a while."

"No way."

"It sounds like he's going to marry her, and we need to support him." His tone was challenging.

"He's too young. I will not allow him to drop out of high school, work construction, and come home to fuck his sprig of a wife in our basement. I just won't." She flipped backward and swam underwater. The water was too warm to cool her temper. She felt more desperate with each breaststroke. When she came up for air, Nick had gone. "Damn that kid," she said.

In the deep end, she bobbed straight up, exhaled all the air from her lungs, and sank to the bottom of the pool. The scapular fluttered in front of and across her face. She grabbed it. Crouching, she felt the sting of chlorine mixed with tears. *I should drown myself. Right now. I did the unthinkable to my lovely son. I spoke my mother's words that used to cut me to the bone. Words I swore I'd never say to my children. I should go to hell for that.* She felt pressure in her chest and temples. *But I can do better. I can apologize to Joey, something Adele never did.* She let go of the scapular, flattened her feet on the bottom of the pool, and propelled herself upward. Bursting through the surface of the water, she grabbed the diving board with one hand and gasped for air. Air that held the energy of second chances.

FRIENDS TO THE RESCUE

Wrapped in a beach towel and dripping water throughout the house, Par went to Joey's room. She tore the July 11 page off the extreme-sports daily calendar that Todd had given him for Christmas. Flipping over the picture of a flying skateboarder, she wrote him a note:

I love you, Joey. Maybe too much. I know you're going through a challenging time, but so am I. You got yourself into a mess, and I know you'll do what you feel is right. I'm very sorry for what I said—about you going to hell. That was mean and uncalled for. Your news stunned me. I hope you can understand. Please forgive me.

Love,

Mom

She taped the note to the cover of his *Harry Potter* book and walked out of his room, wishing she had a magic wand.

Par called Carmen and, before greetings were exchanged, blurted, "I'm having a nervous breakdown again!"

"What now?"

Chilled by the air-conditioning, Par walked onto the patio, looked at Joey's monster-size water gun, then swiftly turned her back to it. "Joey got P. C. pregnant." There—it was said. The sound of the words dripped away slowly, as if hanging tight to the humidity of the day.

"Oh dear."

"I'm set up to win this tournament, and I keep getting news that puts me into a spin." She slapped the back pillow of a lawn chair.

"Calm down, Par. Breathe."

"He's too young for this. He might not even finish high school." She started to walk around the pool.

"Don't jump to conclusions yet. They have options."

She stopped and whispered, "I'm not ready to be a grandma, Carmen."

A pregnant pause. "Yeah, I'm with you on that."

"I always thought you'd be the first."

"Forget that. Ethan's too busy with his studies to have a full-time girlfriend. But he has managed to date three girls, off and on. Two of them want a commitment, but they still make themselves available to him."

"Does he use protection?"

"He says all the girls are on the Pill."

"Damn, I wish P. C. had been on the Pill. I would have taken her to the doctor myself."

"Want me to come over?"

"Yes. I'll be in the pool."

In the changing room, Par put on her rarely used purple one-piece swimsuit. She tossed a lime-green air mattress into the pool and climbed onto it for a float.

About twenty minutes later, Carmen arrived. "Nice to see you dressed for the occasion."

"Didn't want to scare you," Par said with a smile, shading her eyes from the sun with her hand. "What'd you bring?"

"Brownies with frosting."

"Oh, you're bad. Put those darlings in the cabana's fridge, then grab a noodle or an air mattress and jump in."

Carmen took off a short-sleeved terry-cloth jacket and went into the cabana. "Pinky will be here in about five minutes," she said over her shoulder.

When Carmen returned to poolside with blue, yellow, and orange flotation noodles, she jumped into the pool, stuck the blue noodle between her legs, and bobbed next to Par. "I love these things." She squirmed a little finding her balance.

"Is Gail coming?"

"No. She's spending time with Jesse."

"She didn't tell him, did she?"

"I asked Pinky, but she seems too upset to answer."

"Great. Those two are in over their heads. Don't you think?"

"I don't know. You don't need to worry about them right now, though. Don't bring Jesse up."

Par swapped her air mattress for the yellow noodle.

"Hey, gals," Pinky said as she walked through the gate.

"Hey. Hope you brought your suit," Par said.

Pinky ran to the diving board, shedding her shirt and shorts, which covered her swimsuit. Knowing what was coming, Par and Carmen moved to the side of the pool. After an impressive cannonball, Pinky grabbed the last noodle, and the three women formed a circle. "Why weren't they practicing some form of birth control?" she asked, finger-combing auburn hair away from her face.

"They were being stupid, reckless teenagers with no thought to the future," Par said. "I feel like a failure."

"For what your son did?" Pinky asked.

"Yeah, and don't give me any psychobabble about it. It's how I feel."

"What would you think of me if Ethan had gotten a girl pregnant?" Carmen asked Par.

"It takes two, you know," Pinky said. "May I offer an uneducated guess as to why Joey, the good boy, got his girlfriend pregnant?"

"As if we could stop you," Par said, splashing water at Pinky.

"I think that when Todd left for college, you felt the first pains of empty-nest syndrome and, in your suffering, unintentionally pulled away from your remaining son, who is also going to leave you at some point." She looked intensely at Par, then at Carmen, and seemed pleased with their rapt attention. "With you pulling away, he felt rejected, his teenage hormones kicked in, his girlfriend comforted him in the best way a teenage boy can be comforted, and in a way his mother never, thank God, could."

"That's a reasonable theory," Carmen said.

"And I'm going to quit calling her Ms. Politically Correct, because she obviously blew it," Pinky said.

"They both blew it," Par said. "You're right. I haven't been paying enough attention to Joey. This should not have happened. Probably *would* not have happened if I wasn't so focused on golf this year. But don't I have a right to a life?"

"A rhetorical question. How'd he tell you, and how did you react?" Pinky asked.

"He told us at dinner after he ate a truckload of food. Just said, 'P. C. is pregnant' and stared at us. Of course, I screwed up royally. I threw my napkin at him while knocking over my chair and yelled that he was going to hell." Par held her head in her hands, bobbled on the noodle, then steadied herself by paddling with flat hands.

"Ah, the Adele in you came out," Pinky said.

"I did better than Adele, though. I wrote him an apology note, and if he comes home tonight, he'll see it."

"Where is he?" Carmen asked.

"Where else? You know, I'd like to go to P. C.'s house right now and give her a piece of my mind." She looked at Pinky in a challenging way. "That dumb girl. I hate her right now. She'll have twins, you know. I just know it."

"I wonder what her parents think," Carmen said.

Par slid off the noodle and swam to the shallow end. She turned to face her friends. "I couldn't care less. That girl had a chance in life. Now she's ruined it."

"Par, getting pregnant in high school doesn't have to wreck a kid's life anymore," Pinky said.

Par swam back to her friends and treaded water. "Joey's acting like he's going to marry her and support his little family by working construction with Nick." She sank underwater and swam to the ladder.

"Would you stay still, please?" Pinky asked.

"I need something cold to drink. Want something?" Par asked.

"Beer," Pinky said.

"Likewise," Carmen said.

Par went into the cabana and came out with three brownies on a plate and three ice-cold Rolling Rocks. Carmen and Pinky slid off their noodles and climbed out of the pool. They sat at a round table.

"Mmm, chocolate and beer. One of my favorite summer pastimes," Carmen said.

Pinky said, "Mine, too. Now, let's go over other options. After everyone gets over the shock of this news, Joey and P. C. will need to decide what they want to do with their lives—and the baby's life. It is their baby."

"Babies. Twins run in her family." Par drank some beer.

Pinky looked at Carmen and raised her index finger. "One, they could choose to have the babies and give them up for adoption. An open or a closed adoption."

Carmen joined in, raising two fingers. "Two, they could marry with parental consent, have the babies, and do the best they can."

"There is no best in this situation," Par said.

"Oh, come on, it's the year 2000, the millennium, for Christ's sake. There isn't such a stigma about teenage pregnancy anymore."

"I failed him." Par finished off her brownie, licked her fingertips.

"No. It's not your fault. It's the hormones. You remember raging teenage hormones. They're especially intense for boys," Carmen said.

"I wonder what Gail's take would be," Par said, looking at Pinky.

"She would list pros and cons for each solution, then make a decision." Pinky looked down and, with thumb and forefinger, picked her swimsuit away from her stomach, then patted it flat. "That's how she handles everything." She stared at her bottle of beer.

"What if she decides not to go through with the pregnancy?" Carmen asked, with a nervous glance at Pinky.

"No. I'm totally against that," Par said.

They had only once discussed abortion. Decades ago, they had supported Pinky's decision to have an abortion because her baby had been conceived after a one-night stand with a handsome drifter.

"It turned out to be the best decision for me, you know," Pinky said.

"I hate thinking about this. If she has the baby, she's a statistic with a bleak future."

"All that unfulfilled potential," Carmen said, shaking her head.

"If they get married, they'll more than likely get divorced. It so quickly wipes out their youth." Par finished her beer. "Makes me feel older, too."

"Don't make this about you, Par."

Par shot Pinky a slit-eyed stare. "You can't understand. You don't have kids."

"You're right, though—this will have them charging into adulthood."

"My God, they are both too young to be parents. Joey should have worn protection. Or P. C. should have been on the Pill. It could so easily have been avoided." Par looked up to the sky.

"Maybe they are both screaming for attention."

"Oh, Pinky, cut the therapy shit. This is real. You can't help it with your armchair psychology. It's a conceived baby, and it's going to ruin lives."

"I need another brownie. Anyone else?" Carmen asked.

Pinky and Par said no thanks.

"So, you wrote him a note. Won't you talk to him tonight?"

"I'm afraid to talk to him. Afraid of what I might say."

"Maybe you two could call a truce and not discuss it until after the tournament."

"That's an idea."

"What's another few days? This could be everyone's time to just think about solutions and consequences. You have at least eight months before the twins come. Or not."

"I'm having a terrible time. Too many changes all at once," Par said.

"Yeah, you kind of wonder what's next, don't you?" Pinky asked.

Carmen returned, massaged Par's neck. "Man, are you tight. Who are you playing tomorrow?"

"Beth Finnegan."

"Will you win?" Carmen asked.

Par squeezed the neck of her bottle and said, "If Beth has too many martinis tonight, and if I get any sleep, maybe I'll win. But that's a huge maybe."

"We'll love you whether you win or lose. For luck, wear this tomorrow," Pinky said, as she removed her "lucky" ankle bracelet and gave it to Par.

Par hooked it around her left ankle and said, "Thank you. I'd die without you guys."

Before Carmen left to go home, she pressed two valerian capsules into Par's hand and said, "Take these if you have trouble sleeping."

"If?"

"Okay, just take them."

* * *

Joey did come home and Par did talk to him. They agreed not to discuss his "situation" until after the tournament. In bed she worried about it and worried about what might happen next. Around two in the morning, she heard Nick get out of bed, grumbling that he couldn't sleep with her twitching and turning.

Par liked routine, liked to be in control, liked to think she was in control, but she couldn't stop or avoid the onslaught of disturbing events. Her arrest was the earthquake. The aftershocks: two of her best friends coupled, her mother with a boyfriend, her son's girlfriend pregnant. She thought, *This has to be the end.*

A VIOLENT PUTT

In the morning, a headache and thoughts of her young son fathering a child rattled Par's psyche. She waited to hear the garage door go up, then down, waited to know the house was empty of Joey and Nick, waited until she could wait no longer, and forced herself out of bed. The valerian might have helped her sleep a little, but it had also left her feeling sluggish, so she dove into the pool for a wake-up swim.

At seven thirty, she walked out of the house. It was already eighty-five degrees, and the air was thick. Her pores went into sweat overdrive.

As she buckled in, she was startled by the cell phone vibrating in her pocket. She saw it was Sheriff Conrad. "Hello."

"Hi, Par. I'm still catching up from a two-week vacation. Went to Key West like a dummy and sweated off fifteen pounds. Anyway, I see Deputy Virgil has done some damage to you."

"Yes. I was not impaired. She had it in for me."

"Do you have a lawyer?"

"Larry Knight. Do you know him?"

"Oh, yeah. He's good. If it's any consolation, I'm putting Deputy Virgil on probation. She's a bit of a kook, and sometimes that works in the department's favor, but I think she's abusing her power with an obsessive focus on DUI arrests. But this is between you and me. Not a word to anyone, okay?"

"Okay, and if you don't know, her boyfriend placed that defaming article about me in the paper."

"So, she gave him the scoop."

"Yes, and if you fire her, please don't say I'm your source."

"I don't even know you."

Par was happy that Sheriff Conrad understood the situation. Dee Dee, the psycho, would get her comeuppance.

Driving to the golf course seemed to drain what little energy she had. Not good. Not the shape Par needed to be in to win. "Damn it all," she said. "Pinky's right." She had gotten distracted by her misery over losing Todd to the bigger world and her dread of feeling the same pain when Joey left for college, so she had pulled away from her youngest boy, her favorite boy, bracing her insides for the inevitable pain of loss, only to lose him sooner. Why did she have such a hard time with change?

* * *

Par looked at the tournament sheet posted on the outside wall of the clubhouse. Georgia came up to her and said, "Heather's a no-show. Look." She pointed to the last bracket. "Naomi posted a forfeit for her. She'll never live that down." Georgia had no sympathy in her voice.

Something about seeing that terrible word, *forfeit*, made Par feel sorry for Heather.

"You don't look so good. Worried about playing Beth?"

"No. I can beat her. I just have a lot of things going on right now. Things that are cruelly disturbing the one week of the year I need things calm."

"Well, any way you slice it, you will have an easier time today than I, the unlucky one who gets to play the new girl. The gay girl." She looked expectantly at Par. "What? No reaction? Didn't you read about her partner relocating to work at MACI?"

"I read it, but it didn't register at the time. Too busy enjoying my own press."

"Well, you got a lot of it."

"So, she's gay."

"Don't you think it's going to be awkward? This is a conservative town, and we don't have any lesbians in this league."

"Georgia. You might think you know everyone in this league, but believe me, sometimes this kind of thing can happen to your best friends."

Georgia flinched as if Par had poked her in an eye. "Oh, I doubt that." She swatted her golf glove at Par's arm.

Par looked her straight in the face and noticed dark smudges under her eyes. "Maybe we both need some strong coffee."

* * *

At the first tee, Par watched Beth Finnegan, in a coordinated pale-blue-and-white Nike outfit, go through the motions she would repeat for the first shot on every hole: two practice swings, tapping the club head four times on the ground behind the ball on its tee, two glances toward the green, and two slight knee bends. Par had to smile at this ritual. She thought about how Beth had grown into her big bones. Ten years ago, fresh out of college, she had been tall and lanky. Now she was tall and large. Her straight blond hair was pulled into a tight ponytail and pushed through the back vent of a U of M ball cap. As she had gained weight in her hips and thighs, her drives had rolled out an extra twenty yards. She was the best fairway wood player Par knew, and she had the guts to incorporate a managed hook into her game, when most golfers strove for a straight ball. She'd start each shot toward the right rough; the ball would gently curve left and land near the center of the fairway or on the green.

Beth clobbered a drive.

"Great shot. I love how you can trust that hook of yours," Par said.

"I know. If it ever failed me, I'd be in big trouble."

After nine holes, Par and Beth had posted identical scores of thirty-eight. Par felt extremely lucky for a score under forty. Beth had birdied nine by sinking a twenty-foot putt to even the match. Par hoped that putt wouldn't switch the momentum to Beth's favor. They bought hot dogs and bottled water, then joined several players at the tenth tee in what had become a bottleneck because Kim Allen had sliced her drive deep into the woods and was taking more than the sanctioned amount of time to look for it. Liz Carlton passed around a baggie full of homemade gorp: raisins, sunflower seeds, coconut flakes, dried apricots, and walnut halves.

"This should help Georgia out. I heard she was two down after nine," Liz said.

"That would show the new girl," Rhonda said.

Par decided to stay quiet on the subject of Kim Allen. She ate a handful of the energy snack and her hot dog, then sat down on the slope of the tee box and repeatedly stabbed a patch of grass with a tee for something to do. She worried the slowdown would break her concentration. Golf was such a slow game. She was often jealous of tennis players because of the quickness, the reactionary shots, of their sport. Competitive tennis players didn't have time before each shot to psych themselves out. Golfers had minutes to ponder all the hazards of the game: sand traps, rough, water, trees, out of bounds, bunkers, uphill or downhill or sidehill lies. As if hazards weren't enough, the time between shots also fueled self-doubt and indecision about what club to use. A golfer had to close out negative thoughts and zone in on one shot at a time with confidence. She had to forget about a missed short putt or an out-of-bounds iron shot and come back with a positive attitude and an improved swing.

Finally, the twosome ahead of Par and Beth teed off. Par stood up and shook her legs to unstick shorts from sweaty thighs. She set her mind to win the tenth hole with a birdie.

But she didn't need that birdie, because Beth's "managed" hook disappeared and her ball flew straight into the woods on ten and into the water on eleven. Teeing off on twelve, Beth showed how flustered she was by waggling the driver over her ball many times. She still tried for her hook, though, and the ball went straight right. "That's it," she said.

After twelve holes, Par was three up and thinking she'd win easily, probably close out the match by fourteen or fifteen.

Before hitting her drive on thirteen, Beth wisely made an adjustment in her stance so as not to play her hook. She hit a booming drive straight down the middle of the fairway.

"There. Problem fixed," she said.

They both turned very serious. Par felt herself pressing. Her grip tightened. Her swing turned stiff and seemed forced; her shots went off the mark. She bogeyed thirteen, her favorite hole. She bogeyed fourteen, matched Beth's pars at fifteen and sixteen, and bogeyed seventeen, that horrid hole.

Beth parred thirteen, fourteen, and seventeen.

There went Par's lead and easy win.

"We're even-steven," Beth said with a big smile.

Par weakly said, "Yes" and motioned for Beth to lead the way up the hill to eighteen. It was so predictable—the player doing well was so damn chipper. Par had fallen into a grumpy funk and didn't want to talk at all. Didn't want to give away how tired she was or show any dread of a sudden-death playoff. She had to win eighteen, had to win it to get into the semifinal round on Thursday. *Relax and attack.* She could not endure another long year of waiting to try again.

They each hit straight drives and second shots that put their balls on the green in regulation. Par thought she had a better chance for birdie because she was closer to the hole. *Relax and attack.*

Beth's fifteen-foot putt rimmed the cup, leaving her with an easy tap-in for par. She groaned.

"That's good," Par said.

Beth picked up her ball, then stood aside to watch Par either end the match or keep it alive.

To clinch the match, Par had to sink her eight-foot birdie putt.

Relax and attack. She set up over the ball, noticed how the Top-Flite XL letters were perfectly etched onto its shiny, white, dimpled cover. Distracted by this inane detail, her mind traveled to a bad place. She knew she'd lose in extra holes. Knew it like she knew her mother was never coming home and she'd be stuck having to sell Adele's house, ship her belongings west, and endure pictures of her on the beach or arm in arm with that stranger Norman. Knew it like she knew she'd love a grandchild in a less protective, less anxious way. Knew it like she knew Nick was having an affair with their neighbor.

That last thought startled Par, and she froze in place. She recalled scenes and dialogue of Nick's going next door to help Natalie Johnson groom poodles, Pomeranians, shih tzus, and other frou-frou dogs. Why hadn't she seen this coming?

She stepped back, away from the ball, as if it were a bomb ready to go off.

"Par, are you okay?"

Beth's voice jarred Par into moving stiffly to readdress her putt. With a quick jerk, she pulled the club back much farther than necessary for the distance. She banged the ball with a wild stroke, hitting it past the cup and off the green. It knocked into the riser of the first step to the veranda of the clubhouse, bounced high, and rolled backward, coming to rest at the edge of a cart path.

Beth gasped as Par race-walked to her car.

* * *

That stroke ended her attempt to win a tenth victory and set an invincible record in the prestigious match-play golf tournament.

That stroke and leaving the golf course made her a rarity in golf—a bad sport.

Par sped out of the parking lot. She drove down Warren Avenue to Spring Arbor Road, gunned the Tahoe, and glanced at the speedometer as the needle bent toward 80, twitched at 100, then hovered over 110. She turned all the vents toward her face and blasted the air conditioner to dry her sweat and tears. Her mind raced, flashed on her efforts at removing dog hair from Nick's clothes before washing them; Joey's facial stubble, his split lip, his terrible news; Pinky and Gail kissing; her mother's short-short hair; her father driving his Corvette; Pete Masterson in his deputy uniform, smiling at her as if she were a gourmet treat. Her thoughts screamed. Natalie Johnson, plump in all the right places, hair in a short Afro, full lips painted dark burgundy, eyebrows plucked into thin arcs like perfect frowns. Nick had mentioned she was all alpha, which was an asset in controlling the dogs she groomed. Her growl of a voice—another asset. Did he want a woman with such a domineering manner?

Change. It was chasing her down. The Tahoe topped out at 130 miles per hour before she caught up with traffic slowing for the merge to M-60. A siren blared. "Oh no, not that lunatic again." She pumped her brakes, swerved a little, pulled over to the side of the road, and jerked to a stop. The police car sped by, heading in the opposite direction.

"A break. A lucky break, for a change." She held her face with her hands. They were icy. She shivered, turned her face away from traffic, and screamed like a madwoman.

The echo frightened her. She opened all the windows to let it out.

Intense heat dissolved her goose bumps. She socked the passenger seat with her fist and told herself to buck up.

* * *

At the intersection of McCain and Spring Arbor, Par stopped behind a new Impala and tried not to fixate on its trunk. Every time she saw the Chevrolet bow-tie emblem paired with the *H* for *Honda* on the back of a car (the new owner of her father's dealership had gone to bed with the "enemy"), she thought of her father: tanned and proud, spending millions of hours greeting and pleasing customers. How he loved to accommodate large families with station wagons, satisfy the newly divorced and budget-conscious with Novas, excite trendsetters with Corvair convertibles (until Nader, the devil, came on the scene), coddle those resisting midlife with Corvettes, support tradesmen with pickup trucks. He sold Camaros to teenagers spoiled by rich parents, Malibus to young couples, and Monte Carlos to the elderly.

Don't think about him, she thought. *The dead can't help.*

Gripping the steering wheel tightly, she sped into the intersection, turning a hard left. "Dad wasn't so perfect. He was a workaholic and a racist. He was self-centered and opinionated," she said in a strong voice. "And his practical jokes were irritating."

She loosened her grip, slowed down to concentrate on her driving, slowed down to consider what these revelations meant, and slowed down to consider the obvious: Henry was long dead. She was alive.

* * *

At home, she stuffed a suitcase with shorts, sleeveless tops, sandals, toiletries, pictures of Todd and Joey taken when each had turned thirteen. They looked so innocent, so awkwardly perched on the edge of everything adult. She crammed in her pillow and snapped the suitcase shut, went for a stash of cash hidden in a winter-coat pocket at the back of her closet, and jammed it into her wallet.

Passing through the bedroom door, she heard the front door open and close. She stood still at the top of the stairs and didn't breathe. Nick climbed the stairs two at a time; his head was inside the gray T-shirt he was stripping off. Bound for the shower, Par guessed. Shirt off, near the landing, he saw Par, stopped, moved back down a step. He looked at the suitcase. "What are you doing?"

"Where's Joey?" she barked.

"I dropped him off at P. C.'s." His hand squeezed his shirt; his arm muscles flexed. "He's afraid of you."

She fought for control, turned to look out the window. She glared at the sloped roof of Natalie Johnson's home. "I'm moving in with Pinky until I can figure out my life."

"What the . . . Why?"

She turned back around. "I know what's going on with you and Natalie." Standing arms akimbo, she glared at him.

He put his shirt back on slowly. Ever so slowly.

Par willed herself to be patient, to let him speak next. But as she stared at the white, serpentine salt stain that zigzagged across his wrinkled T-shirt, she couldn't help blurting out, "I'm leaving you."

He blinked rapidly; then his arms stabbed the air around him as he said, "I knew about you and Pete. I'd have had to be unconscious not to know you were screwing him. And mourning for him after he was killed. For some weird reason, I felt sorry for you." His face filled red.

"Is this payback?"

"I don't know what it is." He clenched his hands into fists.

She fought a reflex to hurl her suitcase into his chest and send him backward down the stairs—to kill him. To actually kill him, this father of her sons, this man she had committed to for life, this man who stirred emotions she did not want to deal with. She now understood how crimes of passion happened. Par squeezed the handle on her suitcase, swiveled on her toes, and nearly fell over as she retreated to the master bathroom, slammed and locked the door, put the toilet-seat cover down, and sat. Sat and waited. Ripped off her sweat-soaked scapular and shoved it into the wastebasket. Waited some more for her murderous rage to quell.

Natalie. Natalie and Nick. Natalie touching him in his private places. Nick touching her plump and private places. Par thought back to their romp in the kitchen nook two days earlier. He had taken her from behind as she'd bent over the small table. They had never used a table as a prop before. Was that how he did it with Natalie?

So, he knew about Pete and had never said a word. "We are so messed up," she said, wishing for a phone in the bathroom to dial 911. Could a crisis-trained dispatcher help a middle-aged woman, so confused in life, figure out what to do next? Par wanted to yell, *My life is in danger!* She'd probably reach Pinky and have to ask for someone else, who'd pry out the details: *My husband is having an affair, my teenage son is going to be a father, my elderly mother has a boyfriend, my golf game sucks, my best friends—women—are sleeping together.*

Who is threatening your life? they would ask.

Par thought about it. *Life. Life is threatening my life, Goddamn it!* Would they send the police? What if Dee Dee Virgil came out? She slid to the floor and rubbed the cotton loops of the bath mat, as if trying to erase the mayhem.

No one could help her except her.

She went up on her knees, grabbed scissors out of a drawer, and cut off her braid near its base, then snipped the braid into thirds and flushed them down the toilet. The jagged ends of hair spread out above her shoulders; she shook her head and felt freedom with the lightness of it. Staring at herself in the mirror, she knew it wasn't the final cut.

APOLOGIES

Moving slowly out of the bathroom, Par was cautious as she stepped into the bedroom. She heard Nick in the basement, beating his drums in accompaniment to "Roundabout," by Yes.

One day, a long time ago, she had asked him to teach her the basics of drumming. He had made it look so easy, but she found it impossible to coordinate her four limbs doing something different—right foot tapping the bass-drum pedal and left foot working the cymbals' pedal, right hand drumming twice with the stick and left hand drumming thrice. She had felt like a spaz and decided to stick with golf.

As Par brought her suitcase downstairs, she considered confronting Nick with questions about his affair. *Were you ever going to tell me? Do you want a divorce? Are you going to tell the boys? Does Natalie's husband know?*

She stopped at the front door and listened closely to Nick's drumming. He kept hitting the rims and dropping his sticks, which happened only when he was drunk or upset.

They were both upset. Her body suddenly felt weak with sadness. She had contributed to their damaged relationship. She must still love him, or she wouldn't have wanted to kill him. With more thoughtfulness toward him than she had allowed in a long time, Par turned and walked down the stairs, toward the loud grooves of the famous track. When Nick saw her, he hit the crash cymbal and let it quiver with his stare.

He was crying.

Par stood still.

As he switched off the music with his remote, he sputtered, "The first time we were together, it was pure lust, an animal attraction that neither of us could stop." He wiped his face with the bottom of his T-shirt, removed his hemp bucket hat, and fingered its frayed rim. "The next time seemed false. And the last time seemed just that. It's not going anywhere, Par. I want to be with you." He hit the cymbal again, then pinched it quiet. "But you don't seem to care about me."

Par felt hit by a brick in the face. She couldn't speak.

"I'm miserable not teaching. Always have been. It got worse when you became a sub and your work stories were fewer. Those stories kept me connected to the kids."

Oh my. I never thought about what my leaving the full-time job might do to you. I am so selfish, Par thought.

"I miss Todd a lot. We should visit him more," Nick said.

"That's a good idea." Par moved toward him.

He sniffled big. "Joey's a man now. When did that happen?"

She went behind the drum set and hugged him. He cried. She cried.

"We aren't happy people," she said.

"We used to be." He swiveled to face her.

She placed a hand on each of his cheeks and looked into his red-rimmed brown eyes. His face had that old, weathered-barn look from years of working outside—and, she had to admit, from sorrow. "Can we ever be again?"

He looked at her with distrust and curiosity. "There's a third-grade opening at Bennett School. And I saved all my stuff." He pointed to plastic containers stacked neatly against one wall, all the way to the ceiling. They held his third-grade manipulatives, books, games, and stuffed animals.

"Probably a little outdated, don't you think?"

"Some of it, yes. But I saved it, so I'll try to use it."

He smiled, and Par didn't want to disagree.

"Go for it. Your family won't like it."

"They'll deal." He put his hands on her hips. "Derrick's sons are interested in the business. He can bring them on, and they won't miss me."

She put her head on his shoulder.

"What about you wanting to live on the lake?" he asked.

"Hmm . . . maybe we could just buy some land on a lake, any lake, and build a cottage for you, me, and a dog."

"You're kidding."

"Nope. The sooner, the better." She pulled back and said, "I'll never be able to face Natalie or her husband."

"Yeah, me, too. New job, new house, new neighbors. We'll start fresh, Par."

"We can try."

"All the labor will be free, and that's the biggest cost. I'll guilt my brothers into helping me." He hugged her, ran his fingers through her short hair. "I like your hair."

She blushed. "Part of the new me."

"Did you win today?"

Par stepped back and slowly shook her head.

"Too bad. I thought this year would be your year."

Par teared up. He pulled her close, and she whispered, "I don't think I can keep this up summer after summer anymore."

"Do you always have to win to be happy?"

She didn't want to answer yes, and she didn't want to say no. Thoughts confused her: *Winning was what made Dad pay attention to me. I felt special.* She pressed her neck to Nick's and said, "I don't know, Nick. I think I've been holding on to the past . . . and the future has come to get me."

"Wow, that sounds right." He shifted their bodies and tipped up her chin. "Maybe part of the new you is learning to play golf for the fun of it and forgetting about the press, the winning or losing, the bad husbands." He smiled and winked.

Par felt exhausted. "I'm sorry, Nick."

He squeezed her as if he never wanted to let go. "I'm sorry, too."

* * *

Nick logged on to the computer to download the third-grade job application. Par felt shaken and needed her friends. She told Nick she had to take care of some "business" and that she'd fill him in later.

When she drove away from the house, the golf-course scene came back to haunt her. She turned right on South Jackson Road and called Casey Carter on his cell phone. She knew he'd be at the course, collecting stories about the matches of the day. Beth would tell him about Par's insane behavior on eighteen and say that she had won by forfeit.

He picked up on the sixth ring. "Casey here." He sounded distracted.

"Casey, it's Par. What are you going to write?"

"Hold on a sec. Beth, I'll be right back."

Par could hear voices and laughter in the background. She wished she were there. Wished she had sunk that last putt to win.

"Are you all right, Par?"

"No. What are you going to write about my match?"

"Don't worry. No one will ever print another disparaging word about you. Even if you kill someone."

Par smiled at that. She had a few people on her list. "But what will you write?"

"That Beth won one up and she's thrilled to be a semifinalist. Now, how are you doing?"

"Terrible. I'm chasing a record I don't have to chase. My record of nine wins should last, don't you think?"

"Definitely. I don't think the youngsters are going to stick around Jackson to threaten it."

"But they'll continue to dominate the finals."

"Not so sure about that. The older gals posted wins today."

"Well, I can't win anymore. Don't quote me, okay?"

"I won't."

"Go back to Beth—she had a good round today and recovered well from losing her trusted hook."

"Yeah, she was just telling me about that. I'll talk to you later."

* * *

Pulling into the driveway of Pinky's blue-green bungalow, Par admired the berm at one side of the front yard. After Pinky's divorce, she "got landscaping," unlike many people who "got religion" after a personal crisis. She had planted a variety of hostas and ferns, hauled in and strategically placed several large rocks. On the other side of the yard, she had installed a small waterfall and stream; their trickling sounds relaxed people as they walked up to her house. It was surrounded by two lace-leaf Japanese maples, pebbles, and mosses of many green hues. A clay Buddha greeted guests with a big smile at the top step of the porch.

Par pressed her thumb into Pinky's doorbell in rapid succession until the door opened wide. Pinky stood with Gail directly behind her. Their mouths gaped, eyes opened monster-wide. "What happened to your hair?" they shrieked.

Par rushed past them and into the family room with Pinky's poodle yapping at her heels. She sat down in the middle of a red-cushioned futon. Pumpkin jumped onto her lap to lick her face. The two friends followed and stood directly in front of her.

"Have you gone mad?" Pinky asked, as she palmed the uneven ends of Par's hair.

"I like it," Gail said, and looped her arm through Pinky's.

"You know how all these changes—bad changes—have been coming at me?"

"Yes, the stuff of life," Pinky said.

"Well, the knockout punch to this horrible week is that Nick is having an affair with our neighbor and I realized it in the middle of a putting stroke on eighteen. Then I did go a little mad. I walked off the course without finishing my round."

"Let's have some wine," Gail said, and went for a bottle and glasses.

"Call Carmen. Get her over here."

Sitting next to Par, Pinky said, "God, I get off work and the emergencies keep coming at me." She grabbed Par's hand and held it in a tight grip. Pumpkin sat on top of their clasped hands. "It's the dog groomer, right?"

"You should have been a detective," Par said.

"Maybe after I retire."

"The Carm will be here soon," Gail said. "It's the dog groomer, right?"

"You guys are too much."

"Sit down, Gail," Pinky said, and told Par not to share all the details about what had happened with Nick until Carmen arrived. So, Par quizzed Gail and Pinky about what was going on with them: Have you ended it? *No.* Where's it going? *We're not sure.* Are you going to tell Jesse? *Not anytime soon.* Do you think that's fair to him? *Oh, come on, Par. As if you told Nick about Pete.* He knew, though. He just told me he knew about Pete.

Silence.

Pinky looked at Gail and asked, "Do you think Jesse knows?"

"No way. He's oblivious," Gail answered emphatically.

"We're very careful, Par," Pinky said.

"Very discreet," Gail added.

"We're best friends. He'd have no reason to suspect anything between us."

"Pinky brought it up with her therapist."

"Hallelujah. What'd she say?" Par asked.

"She didn't seem surprised," Pinky said.

"It happens, Par," Gail said.

"She said attraction is complicated. Very chemical and sometimes oddly irrational."

Par twisted a button.

"I told her that we're a little confused."

"But happy, too," Gail said.

"That just adds to the confusion," Pinky said, and squeezed Gail's hand.

"I still don't understand it," Par said.

"Sexuality is complex, Par. There's a human-sexuality class at the college. The textbook is two inches thick," Gail said.

"So?"

"Well, it shows you that sexuality—hetero, homo, bi, and everything in between—is more varied than people think. If they choose to think about it."

"Are you manipulating me?"

"Par. This is Gail's reasoned argument. Just listen."

"Here's a comparison for you. People don't understand physics or solar power, but they can accept their existence without taking a class or buying a system."

"Dancing in the Street" rang out. They all looked at Par's purse.

"Ah, a reprieve from this confusing topic." She answered her phone. It was Casey Carter.

"I know something that might be a refreshing option for you, Par."

"Tell me." Par stood up and walked into the kitchen.

"Stacy Calafonti, the women's golf coach at Albion College, is leaving for a job at Arizona State. A big step up for her. I'm writing the story."

Par loosened her grip on the stem of her wineglass. She looked out the window above the kitchen sink and saw tomatoes hanging heavy on their stems, two rows of sweet corn (five feet high and ready to be shucked, cooked, buttered, savored), and sprawling vines of cucumbers and cantaloupes in Pinky's backyard garden. Her mouth started to water. She loved the foods of summer.

"I need an ending for my story. I'd like to close with who her replacement would be."

Par did not know what to say. She inspected the refrigerator. Pinky's dairy shelf was jammed with yogurt, stacks of stinky cheese wrapped in wax paper, cartons of chocolate milk. The next shelf held kosher all-beef hot dogs and plates filled with grilled hamburgers, cooked drumsticks, and trout fillets.

"Got any ideas?" Casey persisted.

The bottom shelf contained a bowl of what looked like homemade vegetable soup and a large salad bowl half-filled with mixed greens, shredded carrots, chunks of green peppers, sunflower seeds. Pinky's manic side popped out to cook one night a week.

"Par?"

"I could think about it for you." She shut the door to the fridge. Was he innocently seeking her help, or did he want to put her name in the story? Could she coach? Would that be a graceful sidestep away from her runner-up reputation, away from her fading talent? The expression "If you can't beat 'em, join 'em" came to mind. She could help the young girls prepare for the LPGA tour, or simply enjoy the college golf scene, as she had done a thousand years ago. Would they hire her?

Casey stayed silent. Par needed to say something to resume the conversation.

"You need to find someone with coaching experience, I'd guess."

"Or someone who's a damn good golfer with college playing experience."

Par thought about her golf coach at MSU—an energetic, supportive woman who inspired the best in her golfers with varied practice sessions and daily motivational quotes. "Casey, I'm at a friend's house. I need to go."

"Par, call me later. I'm not letting you off the hook so easily."

"Nice pun."

"Sure. Now call me sooner rather than later. I'm driven by deadlines."

"Later."

Click.

Par returned to her friends, and plopped down on the futon.

"Who was that?" Pinky asked.

The doorbell rang. Par waved the question aside. The yapping started again. Gail picked up Pumpkin and cooed at her to be quiet. Carmen walked into the room, carrying two large pizza boxes and a gallon of butter-pecan ice cream balanced on the top box. She stopped abruptly when she saw Par. The ice cream dropped to the floor with a thud.

They all looked at the casualty—lid damaged, ice cream oozing. The dog squirmed out of Gail's arms. Carmen jerked her head up and asked Pinky and Gail, "Who's the new girl?"

They laughed.

"Good thing I have hardwood floors," Pinky said as she scooped up the container and fixed its top. Pumpkin licked the area clean, then settled in her doggie bed.

"Get that in the fridge, quick. It must be a hundred degrees out there," Carmen said.

Par told Carmen about Nick's affair. She simply said, "Touché, Nick."

"That's right," Par agreed. "How mad can I be at him? I'm no angel. And he knew about Pete but never said anything."

"Why would he do that?" Carmen asked.

"He hates confrontation," Pinky said, walking back into the room.

Par sipped her wine. "He should never have stopped teaching. I supported the career change and liked the money construction brought in, but it did a lot of damage."

"That's why he became such a big drinker," Gail said.

"He's as upset as I've been with Todd away at school and Joey growing up."

"Jesus, you two need to talk more," Pinky said.

"I've been selfish."

"And obsessed with your golf," Gail said.

"Well, it's time to let go of my need to win all the time."

"None of us is getting any younger," Carmen said, as she moved behind Par to massage her shoulders. "I take it you lost today."

"Yes. I let the outside in and totally lost control. Then I almost killed myself driving like a fool."

"Self-destructive. That's scary, Par," Pinky said.

"That part's over." Par sat on her hands to avoid twisting a button. "You know, my dad loved seeing the press I got through golf, and I thought it made him love me more. I had a thought on my way over here that I'm addicted to positive press because it made him pay attention to me."

"He's gone." A simultaneous comment from Par's friends.

"Yeah, and the dead can't help."

"Wow. I'll drink to that," Carmen said.

After the clinking of wineglasses, Carmen resumed her massage of Par's neck.

"Oh, that feels good."

"You're looser than usual."

Par lowered her head. "I can't imagine life without Nick, but I'm not sure if we can be good together again."

"Try to remember what brought you two together," Pinky said.

"Teaching brought us together."

"Also, you were on the rebound after losing your father."

"That, and Nick was my consolation prize for not going to LPGA Q-School."

"Come on, what'd you two have in common?"

Par twisted a button and admitted they loved being around kids, they were homebodies, they loved dogs, and both had been scarred by death. Out of five boys, Nick looked the most like his younger brother, Sam, who died in a house fire while at an overnighter with his best friend in 1965. At eighteen, Nick had grown a thick black beard to cover the likeness that haunted his parents and irritated his brothers.

"There might be new interests you two can come up with."

"You'll have summers off to travel, maybe camp, hike, have sex in the woods," Carmen offered.

"Maybe so," Par said.

"I don't think you had much in common with Pete," Pinky said.

"That's probably true. Pete was a risk taker. He thrived on the excitement of working nights cruising high-crime neighborhoods."

"He was an adrenaline junkie."

"True. If he had been a doctor, he'd have worked in the emergency room. If he had been a teacher, he'd have worked in an inner-city school in Detroit."

"But he was a deputy, and a good one. Be glad you aren't a widow. I bet you can find a spark to spice up your marriage."

"Ever the optimist, Pinky, and I love you for it. Some good news is, Nick's going after a third-grade opening at Bennett School. I'm sure he'll get it. They always need male teachers."

"I'll drink to that," Pinky said.

Carmen went back to her seat. "Let's eat."

"Even if it doesn't work out, at least you'll know you tried," Gail said.

"And I have started to change. Look at this haircut." She tipped her head to each shoulder, and the uneven hair swayed.

"It's a start, girlfriend," Pinky said.

Par nodded and smiled.

"What's next?" Gail asked.

"Let's eat," Carmen said.

"I'm going to visit P. C. and her parents tonight. I want to feel them out. She is their kid."

Nods of agreement.

"They have more to say about what she does or how she lives than I do. But I don't want Joey to ruin his life."

"Want us to go with you?" Pinky asked.

"Not until after we eat," Carmen said, with a surge of force.

"No. I need to do this alone."

"Try not to be sarcastic or judgmental," Gail said.

"Right. I'll try to be mature." Par sipped her wine with a serious expression and looked at the floor. "I hope those two kids know there are several lives at stake."

"I'm going to lose ten pounds right here, right now," Carmen said.

"Okay, okay." Pinky served the veggie and Mediterranean pizzas.

After big bowls of ice cream, they took a picture of Par and helped her compose an e-mail:

Dear Joy,

Check out the attached picture. I owe you a hundred (remember our bet about the first to cut her hair?). You'll have to come and get it. Tell Mom to stay out there as long as she wants. I'll take care of the Normans. By the way, you're going to be a great-aunt, and Mom a great-grandmother—compliments of Joseph Henry Parker-Swink.

Love,

Par

"This should stir them up a bit," Par said as she tapped Send. For the first time in years, she felt powerful.

THE GIRLFRIEND

As Par drove down Fourth Street toward Prospect, questions for P. C. simmered inside her. *How could you let this happen? What will this do to your bright and brainy future? Where will you raise this child, my grandchild? When will you and Joey ever have a chance to create an adult relationship separate from the demands of a screaming baby or babies?*

Maybe she could choose different words to be more diplomatic.

She was relieved not to see Joey's car at P. C.'s house and drove slowly into the driveway. A pogo stick leaned against the garage door. Two old tires in the front yard spilled sand and were loaded with toys. Scanning the front of the house, she saw brown paint peeling to show splotches of gray underneath. The front door's screen was ripped, and half of it drooped. She wondered why they didn't cut the screen away to eliminate the look of disrepair. She wondered why they didn't mow the damn lawn.

Par hadn't been to the house since last Christmas Eve, and without the pristine snow on the lawn, shrubs, and roof, the place looked like an Appalachian shack. Not that she was an expert on Appalachian shacks, but it was the first thing she imagined.

She took a deep breath.

The stoops of the duplex next door had collapsed risers that left the treads tilted right. NO TRESPASSING signs had been tacked on each front door. An elderly woman, thin and toothless, sat on a metal chair in the front yard, watching two boys, about eight and twelve, play Frisbee. P. C.'s other neighbor had boarded up all the second-floor windows. Knocked out? Shot out? Par couldn't imagine the heat stored in that top floor.

A door squeaked open. She flicked her eyes back to P. C.'s house. Fear hijacked her nerves. She twisted a button. P. C. walked out of the house, followed by four younger girls—two sets of twins in pixie haircuts, dressed identically—one set in pink shorts and white tank tops, the younger set in yellow shorts and topless. They were skinny, barefoot girls with bony knees and darkly tanned skin (a sharp contrast with P. C.'s pale complexion). The door slammed shut. The twins all charged the tire sandboxes, laughing hysterically. They did not notice Par in her car. But P. C. saw her, and with typical firstborn aggressiveness, she walked right up to the side of the Tahoe.

Par looked at P. C.'s small frame and imagined her belly protruding with the grandchild, imagined a small wind at P. C.'s back making her tip forward into a fall. Did this young girl have the strength to carry and birth babies?

"Hello," P. C. said. Her hazel eyes, below modestly plucked eyebrows, met Par's, then shifted slightly left to right. There was a look of curiosity and toughness in this small-framed girl's face that

Par knew would take her far. She knew that P. C. Morgan would not let babies and a smitten boy of seventeen block her from the career path she had set for herself.

Par felt self-conscious about her bad haircut and confused about what to do. Before turning off the car, she pressed her finger into the button to roll down her window.

Their connected glance made Par uncomfortable.

"You're not a twin," Par said, as she switched her glance to the four small girls playing.

"I was. My twin sister died at birth." P. C. hugged the journal she carried everywhere. On its back, she had written *We are what we pretend to be, so we must be careful about what we pretend to be. —Kurt Vonnegut*

"Oh, I'm sorry," Par mumbled. She wanted to leave.

P. C. dropped her arms to her sides.

Par studied her sky-blue, self-designed T-shirt:

Make Cupcakes
Not War

Beneath this message, P. C. had embroidered colorful wildflowers sprouting from the tops of chocolate cupcakes.

Completely disarmed by the goodness of these words, the confidence and potential of this disadvantaged girl, Par said, "That is a very cool shirt."

Startled by the compliment, P. C. stepped back and looked down at the front of her shirt. "I forgot what I put on this morning. Thanks." She glanced at her sisters, who waved at her with goofy looks. Then she said to Par, "Want to meet my beastly sisters?"

While meeting Dixie and Dolly, Tanya and Tammy, Par tried to see differences in the twins. She studied each pair, looking for something different—a longer face, wider nose, different lip fullness, or discrepancies in height and weight. But these pairs had the same wide and round faces, with the exact same features and the white-white teeth of youth. Their bodies were carbon copies of each other.

Par shook their small hands, bent down to be closer to their eye level. "Who's the pogo-stick rider?" she asked.

"I am," all four said at once. They raced one another to the garage, and one of the older twins, Tanya or Tammy, reached it first and started bouncing on the driveway in front of Par's car. They all looked at her for attention.

She clapped.

"Don't encourage them," P. C. said in a good-natured way.

"I'm seeing double. Do you ever get over that?"

"Not really, but they have different voices and personalities, so I can almost always tell them apart."

Par smiled. She had lost the desire to enter P. C.'s home and confront Mr. and Mrs. Morgan about their oldest daughter's "situation."

As if reading Par's mind, P. C. said, "Do you want to come inside and meet my parents?"

"No." Par put her hands in her pockets (she needed the remaining buttons on her blouse). "Thanks, but no. . . . I thought I did, but frankly . . . you know, those beer cans on your Christmas tree . . . it turned me against them right away."

"You're not over that?"

"No, I guess not."

"My parents have problems, Mrs. Swink."

Par nodded.

"Didn't your parents have problems? Don't you have problems?"

The girl made her think. She remembered some of her parents' toxic arguments and knew her own marital troubles had peaked. Instead of being defensive, as was her natural instinct, she simply answered, "Yes and yes."

P. C. touched Par's shoulder and said, "Problems connect the human race, Mrs. Swink."

This girl seemed more insightful than was normal for a teenager. Maybe she should become a therapist.

"I know you're upset. I am, too," P. C. said.

"What about your parents? What are they saying, or recommending?"

"They're angry at me. They think I've ruined my life."

"What do you think?"

"I blew it, but I think I can get through this folly. I won't keep the babies. They'll be twins, you know. Girls. I'm sure of it." She waved her hand, as if to present the four pieces of evidence playing on the driveway and in the yard. "I'll give them up for adoption. I have to. I can't let this stop Joey and me from living out our dreams."

"Well, I know your dreams, but Joey hasn't figured out anything yet."

"Actually, he has, Mrs. Swink. He wants to work with your husband for a year and save his money; then he and I want to backpack through Europe before we go to college."

"You're kidding. I've never heard him say that."

"Have you asked him lately? You know, talked to him about his goals?"

"No, of course I haven't. I've been obsessed with setting a golf record, which I just made impossible today by some terrible behavior on the course. Like you, I blew it."

"Do you think you can recover?" this very smart girl asked. There was no judgment in her words, no rancor. There was only hope.

Par heard honky-tonk music and heartbreak lyrics coming from the house. "Yes, I believe I can."

She left P. C. with mixed emotions about her giving up the babies. She knew the next nine months would be difficult for P. C., Joey, and both families. She felt uneasy that the end to this story was still unpredictable, in spite of P. C.'s commitment to her goals.

When she arrived home, Joey and Nick were playing Ping-Pong. They had moved the table from the cabana to the patio. She watched them from the kitchen nook. Shirtless and in shorts, father and son's similarities were noticeable—long torso, slim hips, a fan of dark hair above the belt line. And differences—Nick's biceps were thicker, Joey's legs thinner, especially at the ankles. They displayed an intermediate level of play, in Par's opinion, and when Joey hit the ball into the pool, she decided to join them.

"Hi, guys."

"Hey. Where've you been?" Nick asked. He gave her a sweaty kiss on her cheek.

"With the girls and the Normans." She smiled at Nick, looked at Joey, and said, "And I went to P. C.'s house."

Joey picked up his towel, stepped onto the coping of the pool. He slowly wiped the sweat off his face and arms. Then he turned to look at her but did not speak.

"I'm starting to like that girl," Par said with honest enthusiasm.

Joey smiled as widely as he possibly could. "Way cool!" he said, then fell sideways into the pool.

"Very big of you, Par," Nick said.

Later that night in bed, Par cuddled next to Nick and said, "When that mother of mine returns and I'm done cat sitting, let's go up north. Just you and me."

"Hmm, sounds good."

"I want you to bring your tool belt."

"Oh, man. That's no vacation for me."

Par felt his body tense. "Not to do any work, silly." She caressed the hair on his abdomen with her fingertips. "And bring a bucket hat for me. We'll go fishing."

"Sounds really good." He crossed a leg over hers.

They slept a deep, comfortable sleep.

LOOSENING THE GRIP

In the morning, Par woke up with the semifinal golf matches on her mind: Beth Finnegan versus Kim Allen, and Rhonda Stein versus Lucy Gutowski. Before doing anything else, she called Beth to apologize for walking off the course the day before.

"Thanks, Par. We were worried about you. Are you all right?"

"I'm getting there. Dealing with a lot of family shockers."

"Let's get together next week for lunch or a drink, if you feel like sharing, and if I win this tournament, I'll buy."

"Sounds good. Good luck today. I hear Kim has done quite a bit of ball searching in the woods."

"Yeah, she's not used to the course yet. Not like you and me."

"I'm going to come out to the course to pick up your back-nine action."

"That's nice of you. Listen, I need to get going."

"Beth?"

"Yes?"

"Do you think I could coach golf?"

A long silence from Beth stirred Par's insecurities.

"Sorry, Par, I turned on the dishwasher and didn't hear you."

"Casey Carter told me about a coaching job at Albion College for the women's golf team. I probably couldn't do it."

"Why not? Those girls would love you."

"Guess I could let go of some of my secrets for hitting a straight ball."

"Just don't share them with Kim."

"Ha. Go and make a bunch of birdies."

Par went for an extralong swim, then prepared a big breakfast: cheese omelet with American fries, bacon, rye toast with blueberry jam, and fresh-squeezed orange juice. As she ate, she realized how gripping tightly to the past and the status quo had diminished her. She was ready to be more attentive to Nick and supportive of Joey and P. C., she was willing to drive north to visit Todd at college more frequently, and she and Nick could rescue a puppy. She smiled at the thought of a playful, energetic, needy, joy-giving, furry new friend.

* * *

At the golf course, Par immediately went into the clubhouse and bought a baseball-style cap with the CASCADES G. C. logo. She adjusted it tight to keep her short, unruly hair behind her ears. Walking down the right side of the fairway on number ten without clubs and without feeling the tension of competition, she experienced nature's calm beauty. The inch-high grass felt like a luxury carpet.

Birds tweeted in the majestic oaks. Undulating bunkers framed the green. Sand in traps was raked smooth like her mother's Zen garden.

Walking toward the bridge to cross over to the twelfth hole, she saw Lucy and Rhonda teeing off. Beth and Kim were on the green ahead of them. Par walked in the rough to get to the thirteenth green and stood near a sand trap. It was hot. She held on to the hem of her shirt and shook it so air billowed underneath. But it was humid air, and she received no relief. Trickles of sweat slid down her rib cage.

Beth, dressed in an all-white outfit, was easy to track. She hit her drive dead center in the fairway, about twenty yards short of Kim's. They both hit the green in regulation and were set up for birdies.

Kim wore her usual black shorts paired with a sleeveless red-checked shirt. As she strolled up to the green, she nodded to Par.

Beth pulled out the flagstick and laid it on the fringe of the green, marked her ball, took off her golf glove, and stuck it in the waistband of her shorts. She walked over to Par. In a low voice, she said, "I'm three up. Can you believe it?"

"Excellent," Par whispered.

"What happened to your hair?"

"Long story. Tell you later. How do you like playing with Kim?"

"I like her. I think she's nervous being the new girl. She's been hitting wild drives, except for this hole."

They went silent as Kim addressed her fifteen-foot putt. Next, they heard the *ping* of connection between putter blade and ball. Par held her breath.

"Damn," Kim said as her ball stopped an inch short of the cup.

"That's good," Beth said to Kim.

Kim picked up her ball, tightened her fist around it. She went to stand near the flagstick with her head down while Beth putted.

Par could relate to Kim's feelings. Leaving the ball short was painful. The adage "never up, never in" haunted golfers.

Beth rammed her eight-footer straight into the hole.

"Nice bird," Kim said.

"Thanks. I'm glad it went in, or the comeback putt would have been long."

Beth winked at Par and gave her the thumbs-up sign.

At the next tee box, as Beth took a practice swing, Par's cell phone rang out from her pocket. She had changed her ring tone to "Chariots of Fire," and it sounded beautiful, but the intrusion was awful.

Beth and Kim jerked their heads to look where the music was coming from.

"Sorry," Par said, and waggled her hand at them. She quickly pulled out her phone and, as she walked back toward the green, muttered to herself, "Thought I had this on vibrate."

Joey, in a loud, high-pitched voice, said, "P. C. is not pregnant! *Not pregnant, Mom!* Her period came this morning. Yesterday she decided against going to the chess tournament; her mom thinks that because she was so nervous about the competition, it made her skip two periods."

"Slow down, Joe."

"Can you believe it? Aren't you happy?"

Her whole body went limp with relief. She sat down.

"Mom?"

From the back of the green, Par watched Lucy in the middle of the thirteenth fairway, dressed in her trademark Hawaiian shirt, matched with a pink visor and lime-green shorts, hit a high shot toward the green. It came up short.

Par whispered, "I am unbelievably happy, honey." What a difference a day made.

Rhonda's second shot hit and bit into the green, rolled backward two feet, and stopped four feet from the hole.

"Mom, are you still there?"

"I am." Her nerves tingled. "Let's celebrate tonight. Invite her over. Hell, invite her whole family over, if you like."

"Really?"

"Sure. If this isn't something to celebrate, then I don't know what is. I'm watching my buddies play golf right now. I think Beth and Rhonda will be finalists tomorrow."

"I wish it was you in the finals."

"Aw, I've had my day."

"Lots of them."

"That's true. I'll see you later." She turned off and pocketed the phone. Watching Lucy and Rhonda approach the green, she somehow mustered the strength to suppress her urge to do a happy dance—a dance with skipping and yelling, arms waving, hands clapping, eyes staring wildly upward, thanking the Big Guy for finally giving her a break.

"Nice to see you out here today," Lucy said.

"Aren't you the good sport, coming out to watch us?" Rhonda said, as she pulled her cart to the right side of the green and took out her putter.

"Thanks. How are you two doing?"

"I'm one down, but if I can sink this putt, we may be even," Rhonda said.

"Hey, I could sink this chip, you know," Lucy said. She bent her head in concentration and hit a pitch-and-run shot toward the hole. The ball smacked into the center of the pin and careened left.

"Wow, nice try," Rhonda said.

But Lucy missed her putt and Rhonda made hers.

They all knew anything could happen with five holes left to play.

Par wished them both good luck. They hadn't said anything about what she had done playing Beth the day before. True friends. Par had plenty to be thankful for. She walked in the rough, cut across the fifteenth fairway, and walked over the bridge. Unable to contain her energy for one more second, she broke into a run as she came to the woods bordering number ten. She weaved around the trees, high-stepped over fallen branches, laughed, and cried. She sniffled hard when she came out of the woods and slowed to a respectable jog as she passed some second-flight golfers on the tenth tee.

At her car, she unhooked a clean towel from her golf bag and wiped the streams of sweat off her face, shoulders, arms, and legs. She needed a drive to settle down before going home. As she sang "Cloud Nine" with the Temptations, the Tahoe automatically cruised over to Dr. Murphy's. There he was, standing near the front of the Corvette, with his arms folded across his chest, body slightly bent at the waist, eyes focused on a headlight. Probably looking for a remnant of a fly's wing.

Par drove into the driveway and parked next to the boxy Bel Air. She smiled at the pair of royal-blue fuzzy dice hanging from its rearview mirror.

As she got out of the car, she said, "Thanks for your letter to the editor."

He pumped her hand with his bony hand. "They truly had no right doing what they did."

"Thanks. I'm slowly getting over it." A dog barked next door, and she looked toward the sound. She felt her conversation on this topic had been used up.

He flicked the long ash off his cigar. She breathed in the wafting smoke. The heat of the day felt hotter as she looked at his paisley ascot, loosely tied and tucked inside the neckband of his short-sleeved oxford shirt.

"I'm glad you stopped by, Par." He buffed the passenger door with a chamois. "If you ever want to take her out for a drive, it's okay with me."

"Really?"

"Yes, but I want to be with you so I make sure you bring it back."

"There's always a catch." She smiled.

He smiled, too. "You'll own her one day. It's in my will, so there'll be no trouble with my kids."

She felt a ripple of shock.

"I've been meaning to tell you. Keep it in your family. It really never should have left Parker ownership. I was selfish on that note."

"It's been good for me, you know. No one should get everything she wants." She shrugged her shoulders, jammed her hands into her pockets, and studied him. He had a kindly face with patches of whiskers missed in his morning shave, a Roman nose with a bump of bone (from playing hockey in college) marring its once-straight bridge, wispy white hair trimmed short. There were dark smudges under his eyes; his gray-tinged complexion concerned her. "How are you feeling?" she asked, fearing the answer.

"Not bad. I can still shoot my age on the golf course."

"Is that eighty-four?"

"You're kind. Eighty-six, and, frankly, I don't want to reach the nineties, in golf or in life. Those aren't bonus years; they're the bitch years. Pardon my language."

"No worries," Par said.

"I'm ready to give it up and join my lovely Belle." He looked skyward with a peaceful expression. "You know, not a day goes by when I don't expect to see her having coffee and doing the *New York Times* crossword puzzle in our breakfast nook. The seven years I've lived without her have been the worst years of my life."

"I can't imagine."

"And you don't have to." He pulled out a handkerchief and wiped sweat off his forehead and neck.

"I will stop by more often, and we can drive around looking cool."

"You're an angel. I'd love that."

Par looked at her Tahoe but didn't want to leave.

Dr. Murphy laughed his little boy's laugh. "Would you give an old man the pleasure of accompanying me for a root beer and hot dog at that anachronistic A&W on Plymouth Ave.?"

Par's mood brightened. "I would love to. My car or yours?"

"Ours. Get in."

He opened the door for Par. Its hinge groaned, and she knew he didn't hear it, or it would have been fixed.

* * *

Before she went into the grocery store to buy food for ten people, Par's muddled thoughts mixed with emotions of sadness, confusion, and some pride. She had survived a week of crazy intensity. How to go forward? She fingered a button and made a decision.

She tapped in Casey Carter's phone number. His phone rang twice. "Yeah?" he said.

"When's the deadline for your article?" Par asked without any preamble.

"Four days," he blurted. "I've drafted the story. Now I'm trying to get some quotes from past and present golf-team members. You have the ending for me?"

"Well, there's no guarantee they'd have me."

"The application is online. Just log on to Albion College's Web site."

"Do you know who else has applied?"

"They'll hire you, Par. I already talked to Owen Hastings, the athletic director. He's a big fan of yours."

"Owen Hastings." Her mind wrestled with the name and a batch of memories. "Ah, he played golf at MSU while I was there." They had played a few rounds of golf together, swapped golf tips, met up at the nineteenth hole after golf meets. What luck. "I'll give it a shot, Casey."

"Perfect. I'm typing it up as we speak." Click.

Par took off her hat and slid fingers through her hair. She pulled the car's visor down, flipped open the mirror, and checked the new style. "Oh, this is bad." She hurled a button out the window. "Bad, and it feels so good."

ACKNOWLEDGMENTS

IT'S BEEN A JOY WRITING THIS NOVEL, and I could not have done it without encouragement and support from the following special people.

Best friends since high school, aka my pack: Deb Boone, Anita Cummings, Nanci Stadel. We've had many adventures together, shared bouts of laughter, and treasured moments. They have been the inspiration for me to write about women's friendships, and were eager readers of early drafts.

Thanks to dear friends, first readers, and experts: Jan Kalahar, Jill and Chet Taraskiewicz, Paul Huffman, Joe Pierce, Paula and Steve Land, Kas Baker, Monica Tackett. Gratitude to Joni Lenkerd for hosting a slumber party celebrating the 50th birthdays of high school girlfriends which kindled an image for the Isadora Fest, and also for the idea of Pringles half-dipped in chocolate; Tina Blade and her brother, Karl, for details about their family's Chevrolet dealership;

Marc Hoffman, photographer and website developer; drummer Peter Igel gave me a beginner's lesson on his drum kit; Gary Kalahar provided insight into newspaper publishing operations; and Annette Fink for the name of a coffee shop, Drips-Drop-In.

For the generosity of information and time, I thank the affable Dan Heyns, former Sheriff of Jackson County. He gave me a tour of the jail, led me through the tunnel connecting to the courthouse, and told me: if you want to write about being handcuffed, you need to be handcuffed. He then took me out to the parking lot where many of his deputies were getting off shift, and had Deputy Dan Deering cuff and stuff me into his car, tell me about field sobriety tests, and other realities of getting arrested and jailed for DUI. Thank you, Deputy Deering. And thanks to the esteemed Hank Zavislak, former Sheriff and Prosecuting Attorney, for introducing me to Sheriff Heyns.

I'm grateful for Kayla Weiner who helped me open doors within myself that I didn't know were there. Much appreciation to the Blue Moon Book Group for enhancing my love of reading through an incredible variety of books, and lively conversations. Big appreciation to members of my writing group who shared stories and taught me so much over 15 years. Thanks to the writers Rebecca Brown, Priscilla Long, and Maria Semple for sharing their skills and insights through teaching courses I attended.

I've been enriched by meeting the kind, accomplished, energized, and energizing Brooke Warner. She and her team at She Writes Press provided fabulous support in helping me realize my dream of being a published novelist.

Thanks to Julie for creating a fabulous place for me to write in our home, bringing in beautiful bouquets of flowers from her garden, and being the one.

© Marc Hoffman/SongbirdPhoto.com

ABOUT THE AUTHOR

KAY DEVELOPED HER WRITING SKILLS by earning certificates in fiction and non-fiction writing from the University of Washington, being part of a writing group, and taking classes at the Hugo House in Seattle.

Kay has a BA in marketing from Michigan State University, and a MBA in management from Golden Gate University. Much of the golf action in this novel was taken from Kay's competitive golf experiences.

When she's not writing, or working on the business of writing, Kay loves to swim, travel, and promote literacy by working as a tutor.

For a Reading Group Guide, or to send a comment to Kay, please visit www.KayRaeChomic.com

SELECTED TITLES FROM SHE WRITES PRESS

She Writes Press is an independent publishing company founded to serve women writers everywhere. Visit us at www.shewritespress.com.

Duck Pond Epiphany by Tracey Barnes Priestley. $16.95, 978-1-938314-24-7. When a mother of four delivers her last child to college, she has to decide what to do next—and her life takes a surprising turn.

Warming Up by Mary Hutchings Reed. $16.95, 978-1-938314-05-6. Unemployed and depressed former musical actress Cecilia Morrison decides to start therapy, hoping it will get her out of her slump—but ultimately it's a teen who cons her out of sixty bucks, not her analyst, who changes her life.

Royal Entertainment by Marni Fechter. $16.95, 978-1-938314-52-0. After being fired from her job for blowing the whistle on her boss, social worker Melody Frank has to adapt to her new life as the assistant to an elite New York party planner.

Our Love Could Light the World by Anne Leigh Parrish. $15.95, 978-1-938314-44-5. Twelve stories depicting a dysfunctional and chaotic—yet lovable—family that has to band together in order to survive.

Hysterical: Anna Freud's Story by Rebecca Coffey. $18.95, 978-1-938314-42-1. An irreverent, fictionalized exploration of the seemingly contradictory life of Anna Freud—told from her point of view.

The Geometry of Love by Jessica Levine. $16.95, 978-1-938314-62-9. Torn between her need for stability and her desire for independence, an aspiring poets grapples with questions of artistic inspiration, erotic love, and infidelity.

CPSIA information can be obtained at www.ICGtesting.com
Printed in the USA
BVOW05s0941130514

353081BV00002B/11/P